He hadn't realized that everyone in town would figure Cara Jane for his girlfriend.

Holt hated that she had been embarrassed by it. He could have prepared her for what she would encounter, but he'd been too intent on getting information out of her to think beyond that.

While walking Cara and her son Ace to his truck, Holt said, "I should've warned you about all that teasing and talk. Everyone knows everyone in Eden, so any newcomer is of interest."

"I understand," Cara replied. Then, looking up at him, she said, "I had a good time tonight. I know I'm a newcomer, but somehow I felt a part of the community."

Eden was a friendly town, and the Watermelon Patch was like one big community dining room. That Cara had felt welcomed warmed Holt's heart.

Books by Arlene James

Steeple Hill Love Inspired

ARLENE JAMES

Arelene James says, "Camp meetings, mission work and church attendance permeate my Oklahoma childhood memories. It was a golden time, which sustains me yet. However, only as a young, widowed mother did I truly begin growing in my personal relationship with the Lord. Through adversity, He has blessed me in countless ways, one of which is a second marriage so loving and romantic it still feels like courtship!"

The author of more than sixty novels, Arlene James now resides outside of Fort Worth, Texas, with her beloved husband. Her need to write is greater than ever, a fact that frankly amazes her, as she's been at it since the eighth grade! She loves to hear from readers and can be reached via her Web site at www.arlenejames.com.

Her Small-Town Hero
Arlene James

Steeple
Hill®

Published by Steeple Hill Books™

STEEPLE HILL BOOKS

Steeple
Hill®

ISBN-13: 978-0-373-87507-8
ISBN-10:   0-373-87507-X

HER SMALL-TOWN HERO

www.SteepleHill.com

Printed in U.S.A.

Nay, in all these things we are more than conquerors through him that loved us.
—*Romans* 8:37

For Dad.
Rancher, builder, oil man, businessman,
salesman, auctioneer…but first and perhaps
foremost, roughneck.
I love you.
DAR

Chapter One

"Right here."

A slender forefinger pecked a tiny spot on the map spread out across the table in the little diner. Outside, rain drizzled down in a gloomy, chilly curtain, holding dawn at bay. Weather reports predicted a continuation of the current pattern of rain for northern Oregon, but Cara's concern centered more on what she would find south and west of here as they worked their way steadily toward Oklahoma and... She leaned forward, checking to be certain that her bleary eyes hadn't played her false. Yes, there, right next to Highway 81. Eden.

Her tired gaze backtracked wistfully the equivalent distance of some thirty miles to Duncan, following the tiny line that represented the silver, two-lane ribbon of road. None of the interminable bus trips of her youth had ever taken her farther than Duncan. She'd originally planned to head straight for the town, thinking that she could find no better place to raise her son than that where she had known her happiest times, but then she'd realized that her brother Eddie would almost certainly think to look for her there.

So Eden it would be. Surely she could find sanctuary in a place with that name.

Next to her in a booster seat on the vinyl bench of the booth, her son, Ace, shoved away the remaining bits of buttered toast that remained from their shared breakfast and rubbed his eyes with two tiny, chubby fists before reaching toward her with a whine. Since his fussing the night before had prevented both of them from getting any real sleep, she knew exactly how he felt, but they dared not tarry another night in the Portland area. She hoped to make Boise, Idaho, before dinnertime and find a quiet motel off the beaten path where she and her little son could rest for the night before driving on.

After quickly folding up the map, Cara reached into the diaper bag that also served as her purse and removed several bills from her wallet. She placed the money on the table before sliding out of the booth, tugging on her short denim jacket and reaching for her son. Their clothing had proven no match for the chilly Oregon weather, but her limited funds prevented any but the most basic purchases. They'd just have to make do with layering. Ace, at least, seemed warm.

He laid his pale head on her shoulder as she reached for the diaper bag. She pulled up the hood of his tiny, gray fleece sweater before carrying him out into the fine rain. After belting him securely into his safety seat in the back of the small, greenish coupe for which she'd traded the minivan deemed suitable by her late husband and in-laws, Cara slid behind the wheel.

She would not regret the loss of the GPS guidance system offered by the minivan or bemoan the state of the eight-year-old foreign car with which she'd replaced it. Instead, she told herself sternly to be thankful for the money she'd made from the trade, cash that, if carefully spent, would help her start a new life for herself and her precious son. Ace would grow up in the safety of a small town, cared for by his mother.

Cara started the car and gripped the steering wheel, suddenly beset by fear and doubt. Gulping, she told herself that she could do this. She'd come this far. She could do whatever she must for the sake of her child and a chance to live a normal, healthy life. With a new year but days away, she vowed that a new life would be her true Christmas gift to her child. He deserved a mother who provided him with a warm, support-ive, affectionate and loving home. That required a strong woman able to make her own way in the world.

If only she knew how to be that woman.

Panic began to swell. Cara knew that she must find a way to protect and provide for her little son or watch him become another possession of his cold, controlling grandparents. But how? The task suddenly seemed too daunting for a woman on her own. Homeless, all but broke and on the run, how could she possibly give her child the life that he deserved and needed? Somehow, for his sake, she must find a way.

Help me! she cried out silently, wondering if her plea could reach through the great void that she felt. God had never seemed quite real to her, but Cara desperately wanted to believe that He existed, that He cared. She wanted to think that her late, beloved great-aunt had been right, that God noticed her distress and would respond to her prayers.

That was not insane. Was it?

She would not think of insanity or the clinic. She would pray instead, though she didn't really know how. Her aunt had always prayed silently with bowed head and folded hands, but the TV preachers sometimes stood with arms upraised, crying out. Surely something in between would work, as well.

Taking a deep breath, Cara whispered, "Dear God, please help me. For Ace. Please help me be what he needs, give him what he needs. Let Eden be just that for us. Amen."

Feeling no calmer but somehow stronger, she sat up a little

straighter, looked into the rearview mirror and shifted the transmission into gear. Guiding the little car out onto the rain-washed street, she fixed her gaze on the road ahead.

Toward Eden and home.

Holt clicked the mouse and watched a new page open on the computer screen before dropping his gaze back to the ledger on the desktop. His grandfather was right. With the occupancy rate continuing high, the motel seemed to be doing well financially. Should they be forced to sell, and provided Holt could bring himself to ask that of his grandfather, they ought to be able to get a good price for it.

The Heavenly Arms had been Hap Jefford's livelihood, not to mention his home, for longer than the thirty-six years that Holt had been breathing. Hap had sunk his life savings into the place and often remarked that the hospitality industry offered the best of all worlds to a man with, as he put it, "the friendly gene." It also offered a great deal of work, most of which Holt's sister Charlotte had managed until Thanksgiving of this year.

Now, at the very end of December, Holt felt like pulling out his hair in frustration. When he and his brother Ryan had encouraged their sister to follow her heart, which meant relocating to Dallas with the man she loved, they had vastly overestimated their ability to handle the added responsibilities here, or even to hire help. Not a single person had replied to the employment ads they'd placed in area newspapers.

Holt pushed a hand through his sandy brown hair, aware that he needed a haircut, but when was he supposed to find time for that? His brother Ryan, a teacher, coach and assistant principal at the local high school, could not be as available as Holt, who was self-employed as an oil driller. Ryan's many duties at the school meant that Holt had to shoulder the lion's share of the work around here. Motel issues now consumed his days, and his own business interests languished as a result.

He'd intended to have a couple new mineral leases signed before the end of the year so he could keep his crews busy exploring for oil, but New Year's Eve had arrived and he still hadn't moved on either one. Heartily sick of changing beds, he told himself that something had to give, and soon. They—*he*—had to have help.

Sighing, he dropped his head into his hands and silently went to the one source that had never failed him.

Lord, I'm stuck between a rock and a hard place here. I don't even know where to look next. There's got to be someone out there who wants this job. Even in this small town, there's got to be someone. Whoever it is, Lord, could You please hurry them along?

A chime accompanied the sound of the front door opening. Holt quickly finished his prayer and moved from the inner office out into the lobby area.

"Hello," said a breathy female voice as he walked through the door behind the counter.

A pretty little blonde in a closely fitted denim jacket worn over a figure-hugging double layer of yellow and white T-shirts stood before him with a baby on her hip, her golden hair curving in a saucy flip just above her shoulders. Deeply set eyes of a soft, cloudy gray regarded him solemnly from beneath gently arched, light brown brows. A pert nose, apple cheeks and a perfectly proportioned, peach-pink mouth in an oval face completed the picture.

Holt walked to the counter and looked down, far down. She stood more than a foot shorter than his six feet and three-and-one-half inches. Hitching the child, a blond, chubby-faced boy, higher on her hip, she shifted her weight slightly and offered a tentative smile.

"Hello," she repeated, dipping her head.

Holt mentally slapped himself, jarring his brain into sluggish activity. "Uh, hello. Uh, looking for a room?"

They had plenty to spare at the moment because of the holiday. The oil field workers who occupied most of the kitchenettes had all gone home to their families, and the truckers who usually filled the smaller units were off the road for the same reason. As a result, only a half-dozen of the twelve units currently held occupants, four by month-to-month renters and two others by out-of-towners visiting friends or family in Eden.

"Umm." The blonde nodded slightly and licked her lips.

"No parties," Holt warned. This being New Year's Eve, he wasn't taking any chances, though something told him he need not be concerned. For one thing, she had a baby with her. For another, she seemed rather shy. He watched her gather her courage.

"Actually, I'm more interested in that Help Wanted sign out there," she said.

Holt rocked back on his heels. He'd never experienced instantaneous answer to prayer before. It almost felt unreal.

So perhaps it was.

He narrowed his eyes while she hurried on in a soft voice.

"I—I'm looking for work, preferably something that would let me bring my boy along. Would this job, maybe, let me do that? I have a baby backpack, and he's used to being carried that way. He's quiet most of the time and…" She swallowed. "Look, I learn fast, and I'll work hard."

Holt didn't know whether to smile or scowl. Two minutes ago he'd prayed for help, and now here stood this strange woman, with a child, no less, and obviously desperate. He felt torn between sending her on her way and hiring her on the spot, a sign of his own desperation. As a man of faith, he couldn't discount the very real possibility that God might have sent her here, however. He stroked his chin, knowing that he had to interview her.

"Okay. First things first, I guess." He reached a hand across the counter. "Name's Holt Jefford."

She ducked her head and slid her tiny hand in and out of his so quickly that it barely registered. Holt took a job application from a cubbyhole beneath the counter. Placing the paper on the counter, he reached for a pen, then realized that the woman couldn't fill in the blanks while holding the boy. He turned the paper to face himself.

"Name?"

"Cara Jane Wynne."

He quickly wrote it out. "Birth date?"

"September first, 1983."

That made her just twenty-five.

"Address?"

She looked away. "The last would be in Oregon, b-but I used to live in Duncan." She slid a sad smile over him. "After my husband died, Oklahoma just seemed a happier place to be."

Widowed and homeless, Holt thought, jolted. *Well, Lord, I knew someone had to need this job.* "Let's use those addresses then."

She rattled them off, and he wrote them down.

"And how long did you live there?"

"Oh, uh, in Oregon, like seven years, I guess, and in Duncan until I was thirteen. Almost fourteen."

He made the appropriate notes, then looked up, but the instant their eyes met, she looked away again. "Job experience?"

Those soft gray eyes came back to his, pleading silently. "I haven't worked since I was in high school," she said in a voice barely above a whisper. "My husband didn't want me to."

"You must have married young," Holt said, without quite meaning to.

She nodded. "Eighteen."

"Ever worked around a motel?"

"No, but I can guess what needs to be done, and I'm not afraid of hard work."

"Can you use a computer?"

"Sure. But it depends on the program."

"Nothing too complicated," he muttered. "But what we really need is housekeeping, someone to clean the rooms, do the laundry and upkeep. And it would really help if you could cook."

A troubled expression crossed her face. "I'm no short-order cook, if that's—"

"No, no, that's not what I mean. See, this is my grandfather's place, and he needs somebody who can fix a decent meal for him at least once a day."

She visibly relaxed. "That I can do."

Nodding, he asked, "Any references?"

Once again, she avoided his gaze. "I don't know… I mean, it's just Ace and me now. M-my husband and I pretty much kept to ourselves."

Holt battled with himself for a moment. His every instinct told him that she was lying to him. A stranger without references or an address, he knew absolutely nothing about her. But she needed the job, and he needed the help. Besides, hadn't he just asked God to send someone? He looked at the baby on her hip and nodded, motioning toward the apartment door. He didn't know how anyone could manage the workload around here with a kid in tow, but that issue could be addressed later.

"Let's go talk it over with Hap."

She walked toward the end of the counter, speaking softly to the boy, who crammed his fist into his mouth and chewed.

She had a petite figure, as those slim jeans showed, and tiny hands and feet, but she moved like a woman.

Stepping past her, he reached for the knob on the door that led into the small apartment where his grandfather lived.

"This way."

Holt Jefford pushed open the door to the apartment and stepped aside to let Cara and Ace pass. A tall, lean man with a ruggedly handsome face and intelligent, olive-green eyes, he made Cara nervous. Perhaps it had to do with the lies. Waves of suspicion had washed over her back in the lobby, but if he suspected that she'd lied, then why would he agree to let her speak to this Hap person?

Cara paused to look around, finding herself in a small private apartment. Unlike the warm, appealing lobby with its wood paneling and black leather furniture, this place appeared a bit dingy and cluttered, from the overstuffed bookcase against one wall to the old-fashioned maple dining set. Yet, it had a certain well-used hominess about it, too.

"Hap uses the front room as the main living area," Holt said, jerking a thumb over his shoulder to indicate the lobby. Three doors opened off the end of this room, which functioned primarily as an oversized dining area. "Bedrooms," Holt supplied succinctly. "Bath in between."

Cara nodded, uncertain why he'd mentioned this, before letting her gaze pick out details. A long narrow kitchen with incongruous stainless steel countertops opened off the wall opposite the door through which they had entered.

The acrid smell of burnt food permeated the air.

"Granddad," Holt called. "Company."

An old man limped into the open doorway, a spatula in hand. The faded denim of his overalls showed grease spatters, and his thinning yellow-white hair stuck up on one side. The two men shared a pronounced resemblance, although age had stooped the shoulders of the elder, whom Cara suspected had once been a redhead.

She found herself musing that this Hap must have been as handsome in his youth as his grandson was now. She met the welcome in those faded green eyes with smiling relief.

"And charming company it is," the old fellow rasped. Cara dipped her chin in acknowledgment, readjusting Ace on her hip.

"Granddad, this is Cara Jane Wynne," Holt said. "My grandfather, Hap Jefford."

Hap Jefford nodded. "Ms. Wynne."

"Cara Jane, please," she said, determined to make that name wholly her own.

At the same time Holt spoke. "She's applying for the job."

Hap's eyebrows climbed upward. "Well, now. That's fine." Hap limped forward, his left hip seeming to bother him some, and smiled down at the child chewing on his fist. "And who's this here?"

Cara hitched her son a little closer. "This is my son, Ace."

"Not a year yet, I'm guessing," the old man said pleasantly.

"He'll be ten months soon."

"Fine-looking boy."

Holt sniffed, and Cara felt a spurt of indignation—until she suddenly became aware of stinging eyes.

"Granddad, did you forget something in the kitchen?"

Jerking around, Hap hobbled through the doorway, Holt on his heels. "Land sakes! I done made a mess of our dinner. Again."

Holt sighed. No wonder he'd asked if she could cook. Cara knew that she had an opportunity here, if she proved brave enough to take it. She lifted her chin and crowded into the narrow room next to Holt, feeling his size and strength keenly.

She tamped down the awareness, concentrating on this chance to prove herself.

"Maybe I can help."

Hap twisted around. "You can cook?"

"I can." She looked pointedly to the skillet, adding, "But it's been a while since I've even seen fried okra."

"Charred okra, you mean," Holt corrected.

Hap handed over the spatula with an expression of pure gratitude. "There's more in the freezer." He gestured at a large piece of sirloin hanging over the edges of a plate on the counter. "Do what you like with that. I set out some cans of sliced taters to heat in the microwave. Opener's in this drawer here. Anything else you need, just nose around. Holt will set the table while me and Ace get acquainted."

"Oh, no. Ace will stay with me," Cara insisted, looking down at her son. Too late, she realized that might have sounded rude, as if she didn't trust the old man. Then again, she didn't trust anyone. How could she? "I—I'm used to working with Ace close by," she said, hoping that would be explanation enough.

Hap traded a look with his grandson, and Cara held her breath until the old man nodded, smiled and said, "You and the boy will join us for dinner, of course." He somehow managed to make it an order without it sounding like one. Cara breathed a silent sigh of relief.

"Thank you."

"No need for that when you're cooking. We'll talk about the job later."

Nodding, Cara told herself not to blow this. It had been months since she'd cooked a meal, but surely she could manage this. Hap hitched himself past her and out into the other room, while Holt remained behind to lean a hip against the counter. Ignoring him, Cara sat Ace on the floor in a corner near what appeared to be the back door and removed his knit hoodie and the sweater beneath it. She took a small wooden toy truck from her jacket pocket and gave it to Ace before looking around her.

The apple-green walls and cabinets of pale, golden wood contrasted sharply with the industrial-grade metal countertop, but everything looked neat and clean if an odd mixture of the old and new, the professional and the homey. Noting the lack of a dishwasher in the small, cramped room, Cara glanced hopefully at the solid door next to the refrigerator.

"That goes out to the laundry room," Holt told her.

So, no dishwasher. She checked the sink. And no garbage disposal. Well, she'd survived a lot of years without those things.

"There's a big coffee can for scraps," he said, pointing to the cabinet beneath the sink. "It goes into the Dumpster out back when it's full. There's extra cans on a shelf above the dryers."

Nodding, Cara got down to work. She went to the freezer compartment of the refrigerator, moving past the tall man who watched her like a hawk. She found the okra in a half-empty plastic bag and a small box of frozen green beans.

"Okay if I use these?"

Holt glanced at the box of green beans, then at the boy now tapping the truck on the floor. "Sure. Use anything you want." With that, he moved to an overhead cabinet and began removing the dinner dishes, taking his time about it.

While Ace banged happily, Cara scraped the blackened okra and grease into the can under the sink, replaced the lid, cleaned the skillet and began looking in cabinets. Finally she asked, "Oil?"

Holt nodded at the tall, narrow cabinet doors across from the refrigerator. "In the pantry. Oh, and, by the way, there's a chance my brother Ryan will be joining us, too."

That meant three Jefford men, not just two, which explained the huge slab of steak. Cara removed her jacket, hoping he wouldn't notice the sleeveless tank tops that she wore in the dead of winter, and started heating the oil in the frying pan.

"Should I set a place for Ace?" Holt asked. "We don't have a high chair."

"No, that's all right," she answered without looking at him. "He'll sit in my lap, eat off my plate."

Holt went out, carrying dishes and flatware.

Cara's hands shook as she reached for the skillet, but a glance at her son stiffened her resolve. She could do this. She had to do this. Everything depended on it.

Chapter Two

Hap sat at the end of the table in his usual chair, reading from his Bible, when Holt carried the dishes to the table. He looked up, waggling his eyebrows and jerking his head toward the kitchen, but Holt didn't know what to make of Cara Jane Wynne yet. Shrugging, he began to deal out the plates onto the bare table. Charlotte had always kept the table covered with a fresh cloth and place mats, like their grandmother before her, but Holt and Hap had quickly found them a deal of work to maintain.

Hap crooked a finger, and Holt stopped what he was doing to lean close. "So? Tell me 'bout her."

"Not much to tell," Holt muttered. "She came in off the street, says she hasn't worked since high school and grew up in Duncan but last lived in Oregon. My guess is she's homeless and desperate." Hap made a compassionate sound from deep in his chest, and Holt frowned. "That doesn't mean she's trust-worthy," he pointed out softly, then stiffened when she spoke from the doorway behind him.

"Excuse me. Are there serving dishes you'd rather I didn't use?"

Hap smiled and shook his head. "Use what you like. She that cooks gets to make the decisions in the kitchen, I always say."

"Okay."

Frowning some more, Holt laid the flatware, then went back to the kitchen to fill three glasses with ice and water.

Holt toyed with the idea of calling his brother to come over and evaluate Cara Jane. The satellite cell phones that their new brother-in-law Ty had given them for Christmas made it much easier to keep in touch, but Ryan often could not be called away from whatever activity currently required his supervision. As an assistant principal, history teacher and all-around coach, Ryan wore many hats. If they saw Ryan tonight at all, it would be briefly.

Holt could have used Ryan's input, but he understood only too well what it meant to be busy. His own drilling business and ranch and now the motel kept him tied up. Maybe, just maybe, Cara Jane was God's answer to that dilemma. He wondered if hoping so made him selfish or if not quite trusting her made him unfair. He didn't want to be either.

He took his time ferrying the glasses from the sink to table, making two trips of it. She never once glanced his way, but he found it difficult to take his eyes off her and the boy, who had pulled himself up and wrapped his chubby little arms around his mother's knees. Was she the poor little widow woman she seemed or something much more dangerous?

Holt felt sure that Cara Jane and Ace Wynne were going to be around until God had accomplished whatever purpose had brought them here. If that meant Holt could soon get back to his own life, so much the better, but he couldn't quite shake the feeling that all was not as it should be with her.

Cara placed the last platter on the table, Ace on her hip, and took a final survey of the meal: golden-fried okra, pan-grilled steak, buttered potatoes, green beans and carrots straight out of the can. Nothing fancy and nothing fresh.

You're not in California anymore, Cara.

Suddenly that warm and sunny place called to her. She'd left with no regret. Nevertheless, she suddenly found herself missing certain aspects of her old life, such as the warmth and sunshine.

Cara pulled out the chair and took a seat at the table, shifting Ace onto her lap.

"Gracious Lord God."

Hap's gravelly voice jolted Cara. She looked around to find the Jefford men with bowed heads. To her shock, Holt and his grandfather had linked hands. More shocking still, each of their free hands rested atop the table as if they'd reached out to her. Embarrassed, she pretended not to notice, holding Ace tight against her midsection and bowing her own head as Hap prayed.

"We thank You for this food and the pretty little gal You sent to cook it up for us. And thank You for bringing our Charlotte and Ty back safe from their honeymoon. We look forward to them coming home. You know we want only their happiness and Your will. Amen."

"Amen," Holt said. "Let's eat."

The two men practically attacked the food.

"My stars!" Hap declared, sliding a piece of pan-grilled steak onto his plate. "Will you look at that." He shot a grin at Cara, displaying a fine set of dentures. "Haven't had a piece of cooked meat I could put a fork in since our Charlotte up and married."

Over the course of the meal, Cara began to have doubts about her cooking, mostly because of this Charlotte of whom they spoke so glowingly. Charlotte, it seemed, was nothing less than a chef. They spoke of "good old country cooking" and such things as dumplings, chitlings and black-eyed peas.

"Speaking of black-eyed peas," Hap said, "good thing we're not superstitious."

"Why is that?" Cara asked idly, pushing Ace's hand away as he grabbed for steak and offering him a piece of carrot instead.

Holt braced both forearms against the tabletop and stared at her. "You grew up in Oklahoma and you haven't heard of eating black-eyed peas on New Year's for good luck?"

Cara dropped her gaze back to her son and tried not to tense, hoping the question would simply pass.

"Would that be New Year's Eve or New Year's Day?" Hap interjected. "Never was sure myself."

Relieved, she poked a green bean into Ace's babbling mouth with her fingers.

Holt stabbed potatoes with his fork, saying, "Well, if you want them for tradition's sake, I'm pretty sure there's a bag in the freezer, and since we don't believe in luck anyway, we might as well have them tomorrow as tonight, you ask me."

"You don't believe in luck?" Cara heard herself ask.

Holt looked up, eyeballing her as if she'd just beamed in from another galaxy. "As Christians, ma'am, we believe that God is in control of our lives, not random luck."

"Oh. I—I see." Except, of course, she didn't. God could not have been in control of her life or it would not have turned out like this.

Hap winked at Cara. "For tradition's sake, then. I like my black-eyed peas. Reckon if you stuck around you could rustle up a mess for us, young lady?"

Cara blinked. "Oh, I, um…"

"If you can cook beans, you can cook peas," Holt put in impatiently. "Just throw in a ham bone and make some corn bread."

"Now, Holt," Hap scolded mildly, "if it was that easy, we'd be doing it our own selves, wouldn't we? 'Sides, maybe she and the boy will be spending the holiday with family. Did you ever think of that?"

"Is that right?" Holt asked her. "You have folks around these parts?"

"No. No, I don't."

"Well, that's a shame," Hap said, shaking his head. "But if you got no family around, what brung you here? If you don't mind my asking, that is."

Cara opened her mouth, but Holt supplied the information before she had a chance to speak.

"Cara's a widow," he announced. "Looking for more cheerful surroundings."

Hap sat back in his chair, wiping his mouth with a paper napkin. "Now, that's a grief that I know too well." He looked Cara in the eye. "Both my wife and my son have passed from this world. You must have some family somewhere, though. They no comfort to you?"

"My parents are both gone," she said, which was technically the truth.

"No brothers or sisters?" Holt asked, sprawling back in his chair, which seemed too small to hold him.

She had the lie ready, but somehow it just wouldn't slide off her tongue. Besides, what harm could there be in at least admitting to Eddie? No doubt he was trying to track her down as they spoke, but the Jeffords wouldn't know that.

"A brother," she said, "but we're not close." Cara smoothed Ace's pale hair lovingly. "It's just us two really."

Hap shook his head. "It's a powerful sorrow when a father leaves a young family behind."

"Yes." Cara laid her cheek against the top of her son's head. "Ace was five weeks old when it happened."

Holt reached out a long arm and laid his fork in his plate. "Mind if I ask how your husband died?"

While she felt the shock that always came with the truth, she carefully masked her emotions. "He fell."

The two men traded looks, and Holt sat up straight again, looking uncomfortable now, his gaze going to Ace as he once more picked up his fork. "That's how my father died, too. He fell off an oil derrick trying to fix a pulley."

Cara took it that Holt's father and Hap's son were one in the same. "They say he didn't suffer," she offered softly, swallowing hard.

Both Holt and Hap nodded at that. Apparently they'd been told the same thing.

"What'd your man fall from?" Hap asked.

"A highway overpass. He stopped to help a stranded motorist and somehow fell over the railing. No one's certain just how it happened," she said, still puzzled, "and the funny thing is, it wasn't like Addison to stop and help a stranger. Not like him at all."

Hap laid a gnarled hand upon her arm. "There are mysteries to which none are privy, and greater mysteries revealed to all. We must trust God with the first and thank Him for the last." Hap looked at Holt.

Cara sensed a certain reluctance in Holt, but she knew the moment had come to discuss business.

"The job requires long hours," he said. "It pays a salary on the first and the fifteenth." Holt glanced at his grandfather. "Plus room and board."

The figure he named didn't amount to much pay, but she wouldn't have to worry about food and shelter. "What about Ace? I need to keep him with me. If it's just housekeeping work, I know I could manage. He won't be any trouble to anyone."

"Well, there's housekeeping and then there's *housekeeping,*" Holt said, and for the next fifteen minutes he detailed all that she would be expected to do.

It seemed overwhelming: beds to be made, laundry to be

done, floors, bathrooms, draperies, dusting, sanitizing, even kitchens in some of the rooms. Every room. Every day. That did not include meal preparation or registering guests from time to time. But it did include Ace.

"We could give it a try," Hap said. "If the work and the boy together prove too much for you, we'll figure something out. It's not like you'd be on your own around here."

"Except for Saturday nights," Holt put in. "I take Granddad out for dinner on Saturday nights."

"Every other," Hap corrected, with another of those teasing winks at Cara. "Me and Charlotte, we always took turns with those Saturday nights. All you'd have to do is hang around here and watch the front desk."

That sounded doable to her. "I take it Charlotte used to work for you?" Cara asked carefully.

Hap chuckled. "Not exactly. Charlotte's my granddaughter, Holt's baby sister. She up and married this rich fellow from Dallas."

"Work she did, though," Holt added. "More than I ever realized until I had to take over her job myself."

"Then essentially I'd be replacing *you?*" Cara exclaimed, pointing. Ace burbled something unintelligible and copied her gesture. Cara quickly pushed both their hands under the table, cheeks heating.

"That's the idea," Holt said dryly. He seemed to doubt she could do it. Just the way he swept his hard gaze over her seemed to pronounce her lacking somehow.

Hap waved a hand. "Now, now. Let's not get ahead of ourselves here." He pointed his fork at Cara. "You and the boy stay the night, take a good look around, think on it, and we'll all pray this thing to a conclusion. How does that sound?"

Cara smiled, feeling cautiously hopeful for the first time in months. "That sounds fine."

"Does that mean we get black-eyed peas tomorrow?" Holt asked, digging into his food again.

"Mmm, maybe some greens, too," Hap said longingly. "There ought to be a can in there. I hope there's a can in there."

"I think I'm not used to the same kind of cooking you're used to eating," Cara confessed.

"Oh, it's simple fare," Hap said, "nothing you can't manage, I reckon."

"It's sure to beat his cooking," Holt said, wagging his fork at Hap.

Hap pretended to take offense, frowning and grinning. "My cooking's what's kept these skin and bones together these past weeks, son, and don't you forget it. How many meals have you cooked since your sister married? Answer me that."

"None," Holt admitted. He grinned at Cara, grooves bracketing his mouth. Suddenly he looked heart-stoppingly attractive, sitting there in his faded chambray shirt that emphasized his strong, wide shoulders. "I like breathing even more than eating," he quipped and went back to doing just that.

"There you are!" Hap declared, slapping a hand lightly against the edge of the table. He looked cajolingly to Cara. "So do we get them black-eyed peas?"

"Black-eyed peas," Cara promised, gulping. "For tradition's sake."

But, oh, she thought, watching Holt chew a big bite of steak, *I could use just a little luck, too.*

Cara looked around the tiny, crowded bedroom with dismay. It still contained much that belonged to its previous owner: books, photos, various other keepsakes, even a yellowed set of crocheted doilies. An old-fashioned four-poster bed, dresser, domed-top trunk and wicker laundry hamper left only a narrow corridor of walking space around the bed.

She felt Holt at her back, watching her judge the room, and fought the urge to curl into a tight little ball. She'd hoped never again to live in someone else's space, meeting their standards rather than her own, always the outsider, never truly belonging or having control of her own life.

Hitching Ace a little higher on her hip, their outer garments clutched in one hand, she bucked up enough courage to say, "I think we'll be more comfortable renting a room for the night."

After a moment of silence, Holt replied, "I'll get a room key for you."

Relieved, Cara watched him stride for the lobby. After she'd taken a look at those frozen black-eyed peas—and thankfully found the preparation a simple matter of stewing in water for an hour or so—Hap had suggested Holt show her where she could stay the night. She'd never expected to be offered a room in the apartment.

A chime sounded as Holt crossed the room. Hap, who was stacking dishes in the kitchen, having insisted on helping her clean up after the meal, exclaimed, "Tell 'em I'll be right out!"

Just then the door opened and two elderly men appeared, their happy voices calling, "We're here!"

One of the newcomers wore dark pants and a white shirt beneath a sweater vest. More portly than the other, he boasted glasses with heavy black frames and a luxurious head of snow-white hair. The other, dressed in denim and flannel, possessed neither. Spying Cara and Ace, they stepped forward.

"Looks like y'all started the party without us," the flannel-shirted man said.

The other elbowed him and, without taking his eyes off Cara, commented, "Justus, your idea of a party is a bag of potato chips and a root beer."

"Yessiree-bob, 'specially if it comes with a purty gal." He nodded at Cara, eyes sparkling.

Holt laughed, and the sound resonated from the top of Cara's head to the very tips of her toes. He looked over one shoulder at her. "This is Teddy Booker and Justus Inman, two of the best domino players around. Otherwise, they're harmless. Fellows, meet Cara Jane Wynne. And the little guy's Ace."

Cara nodded, and the men nodded back, speculation lighting their eyes.

The chime came again, and Holt looked past them into the outer room. "Land sakes, Marie," he said, going forward, "is all that food? Come here and let me kiss your feet."

General laughter followed, during which a woman remarked, "Well, I know you poor things are still missing Charlotte, and it's no party without fixings."

Holt went out into the other room, followed by Misters Booker and Inman. Holt seemed an altogether different fellow than the one she'd known thus far, Cara mused. Why, he could be downright charming when he wanted to be.

She carried Ace to the table and began dressing them both for the outside. She'd tossed on her own jacket and had just pulled the sweater over Ace's head when Hap hitched his way into the dining area, grinning happily.

"We're having a few friends in for dominoes," he announced. "That's our chief pastime around here. Figured we might as well usher out the old year that way. You two are welcome to join us."

"Oh. No, thank you," Cara refused quickly, stuffing a little arm into a sleeve. "He needs a bath and then bed." The ripe smell of her son told her that he was more than ready for a fresh diaper, too.

"I have your room key right here," Holt said, reappearing. He looked to Hap. "Cara Jane thinks she'd be more comfortable in a rental unit tonight."

"Sure," Hap agreed, heading off to join his guests. "No

charge, on account of that dinner. We got plenty of space, and these jokers do tend to be a mite loud. You change your mind about the party, though," he told her, "you come on over, you hear?"

Cara nodded and smiled, tugging Ace's sweater down. Hap disappeared into the other room, where someone shouted, "Let the games begin!"

Holt closed the door behind him, saying, "I'm going to put you in Number Six. There's just one bed and more room for the portable crib that way."

"That's fine," Cara said, wrapping Ace's jacket around him and gathering him against her chest. She'd found sharing a bed with her little son like sleeping with a whirling dervish. Pleased with the unexpected luxury of a crib, she reached for the key.

To her surprise, Holt slid it into his pocket before grabbing his coat from a peg on the wall. "I'll just see you settled in."

"That's not necessary. I don't want to keep you from your guests."

"Hap's guests," he said, shrugging on the leather-trimmed canvas coat. "They've got enough to make up a table. They won't miss me." He lifted a brown cowboy hat from another peg and fitted it onto his head, suddenly seeming ten feet tall. Nodding toward the kitchen, he said, "We can go out through the back."

Cara put on a smile and moved ahead of him, holding Ace closer to her chest to keep him warm. He babbled in a singsong voice to himself as they stepped out onto the pavement, cold enveloping them.

Shivering, Cara hurried ahead of Holt to the car parked beneath the drive-though. At least, she told herself, they'd gotten a meal out of this and would sleep warm tonight. Tomorrow would just have to take care of itself.

Chapter Three

"I'll, um, move the car later, if you don't mind," Cara Jane said.

Holt shrugged. It seemed odd to him to leave the car sitting there under the drive-through, but a great deal seemed odd about Cara Jane Wynne. He reached into the trunk of her car for the two bags there.

"You can park your car in that space just to the left of the door to your room," Holt told her, hoisting their two bags. Neither of them, he noted, weighed enough to tax a child, let alone a grown man. A wise woman wouldn't pack more than she could tote herself, but Holt figured that starting a new life would require a great deal more than Cara Jane seemed to be carrying.

All that remained in the trunk was a lightweight baby backpack, which told him just how Cara Jane intended to manage her son while she worked. Trying to do such work with a baby strapped to her back seemed foolish to him, but he supposed she'd figure that out soon enough.

While he carried their bags to the room, Cara Jane closed the trunk lid and went to rummage around in the car.

Opening the door, Holt entered and hit the light switch with his elbow. Leaving the door slightly ajar, he hoisted the bags onto the long, low dresser, then went to turn on the heat. The place could best be described as utilitarian, he supposed, but at least it was clean and neat.

She came in moments later carrying Ace, a stuffed diaper bag and a small plastic tub of groceries. Holt took the tub from her and closed the door so the place would warm up. Already the air that blew from the vent above the closet felt toasty enough to take the immediate chill off.

"Should be comfortable in here soon," he told her. Nodding, she dropped the diaper bag on the bed and turned to face him. "Furniture's bolted down," he informed her.

She shrugged. "Safer that way. Ace likes to pull up on whatever he can find."

"You're traveling light," Holt commented, waving a hand at the suitcases.

"I live light," she replied.

He had no idea what that meant, but he intended to make sure that she had a clear picture of what she would be getting into if Hap hired her. "A job like this requires hard work," he told her. "Take it from me."

"I understand."

"I'm not trying to discourage you, and God knows we can use the help. I just want you to be aware of what you'd be getting into."

"I appreciate that."

"I'm not sure you can," he said, rubbing his ear. "You and the boy want to come along, I'll show you one of the kitchenettes so you can get a better idea of what you'd be up against."

For a moment, he thought she might refuse. He had to admit that if he was standing here in nothing more than a jean jacket, he might have balked himself. Where, he wondered, was her coat? Didn't they wear coats in Oregon?

Cara nodded, held the boy close and headed for the door. Holt followed her out, pulling the door shut behind him and trying not to watch the sway of her hips.

Holt used his passkey to let them in the room next door and snapped on the light. The kitchenettes basically contained two rooms, pass-through closet and bath in one, bed, sitting area and tiny kitchen in the other. Cara stood in the center of the room, the boy on her hip, and looked around. Holt couldn't help noticing the way her eyes lit at the sight of that puny kitchen. Then she swept her fingertips along the arm of the tweedy sofa.

"It makes into a bed," he told her, "but because of the lack of space, it's usually folded up when we get here to clean, so you always have to check the sheets, even if only one person is supposed to be in the room."

"I see."

"Then there's the kitchens," he went on. "The regulars usually do their own dishes, but if they don't, you have to. The kitchens have to be meticulously cleaned to keep the bugs out."

"Good policy."

"Half our units are kitchenettes," he pointed out, wanting to ruffle her for some reason. "The rugs have to be cleaned periodically, as well as the draperies."

"All right."

"Look," he said, "I'm an old roughneck, and I'm telling you, it's hard work."

She turned on him, her face stony. "Okay, I get it. You don't think I can handle the job."

"I didn't say that. I just want you—"

"To know what I'm getting into," she finished for him, brushing by on her way to the door. "Yeah, yeah."

Irritated, he caught her by the crook of the elbow. "I just think you should have all the facts before you make your decision."

She jerked her gaze up at him. "Are you saying that the job is mine if I want it?"

For an instant, he felt as if he might tumble headfirst into those soft gray eyes. Abruptly, he released her and stepped back, clearing his throat. "I'm saying you should be fully informed. The rest is between you and Hap."

She flicked a doubtful glance over him and walked out into the cold night. He didn't blame her for not buying that. She, however, didn't know Hap. If Hap made up his mind to take her on, nothing his grandsons could say would make any difference, not that Holt wouldn't dig in his heels if he thought he should. He just hadn't really decided yet whether or not he would.

On one hand, Holt badly wanted the help she could provide. On the other, something wasn't right about her. Too pretty, too alone, too quiet, she set his every sense on alert.

He wondered, as he fetched the portable crib and hauled it over to her room, just how he might go about running a background check on her. They'd never had to worry about things like background checks before, though Ty had suggested they consider it. Holt would speak with his brother-in-law about it. Meanwhile, he'd keep a close eye on Cara Jane Wynne.

Cara rolled onto her stomach and folded her arm beneath the pillow under her head, listening to the faint whir of the heater and Ace's easy breathing. He'd objected when she'd belted him into his car seat and moved the car after Holt had gone back into the apartment, but she hadn't wanted Holt to hear the awful knocking racket that her old car had started making earlier in the day. She couldn't help feeling foolish for having traded her dependable, almost new minivan for an older, high-mileage car, but she'd desperately needed the cash, which hadn't gone as far as she'd hoped. She certainly didn't want to give Holt Jefford a reason to question her good sense, so she'd waited until he'd gone to move the car.

After his bath, Ace had sucked down a bottle of formula then dropped off to sleep in no time, but she had not been able to. A giant clock in the distance seemed to be counting off the minutes—*ka-shunk, ka-shunk, ka-shunk*—while her mind whirled with the possibility of working for the Jeffords and all it involved. She kept thinking, too, about the kitchenette next door and imagining herself sitting down to that little bar with her son. It would almost be like having their very own place.

Cara thought back to her bitter disappointment upon realizing, on the heels of her husband's death, that the house in southern California had not belonged to her and Ace. Learning that it had been sold out from under her had sent her into a sharp decline.

Rolling onto her back, Cara cut off that line of thought. She and Ace were together and free of the past, and it was going to stay that way. No matter what she had to do, she would prove herself capable of making a good life for her son.

Provided she could make this job work for them.

Holt worried her. She couldn't escape the fear that he knew she'd lied. Thankfully the old man seemed more trusting. She'd prefer to concentrate on him, but she sensed that she must convince Holt, too, if she had any chance of staying on here.

Recalling words that Hap had spoken during dinner, she sat up and wrapped her arms around her bent knees. She felt the lonely weight of the darkness, heard the relentless *ka-shunk, ka-shunk* of an invisible machine and let the curious words wash over her.

"There are mysteries to which none are privy, and greater

mysteries revealed to all. We must trust God with the first and thank Him for the last."

What had he meant by that? She would never understand Addison's death, but what "greater mystery" had been or would be "revealed to all" and why should anyone give thanks for it? She had never heard her aunt speak of such things, but no doubt the Jeffords could tell her. They seemed to be devout Christians, which only made her dishonesty seem worse, but she had to protect herself and her son.

"We believe that God is in control of our lives, not random luck."

Had God, she wondered, brought her here? She'd been praying a lot lately, and this certainly seemed the perfect place for her and Ace. For one thing, no one would think to look for them in the Heavenly Arms Motel in Eden, Oklahoma. Plus, this job offered not only a modest salary but shelter and food, as well, and the Jeffords seemed willing to let her keep Ace with her while she worked. If she could convince them to let her and Ace stay in one of the kitchenettes, it would be very nearly perfect, no matter how difficult the job might be.

Besides, she had the feeling that she might find answers here, answers to questions she didn't even know to ask yet.

If only she had the chance. If Holt would give her the chance.

Laughter filtered in from outside.

Feeling terribly alone, Cara glanced at the clock and saw that the old year had passed. *Ka-shunk, ka-shunk, ka-shunk.* Closing her eyes, she did what Hap had suggested and said a prayer.

Please let this work out for us. Please let this be the start of a new life, a real life, for us.

Needing reassurance, she leaned far to the side and peered over the edge of the crib at her sleeping son. "Happy New Year, sweetheart," she whispered.

Ace slept on undisturbed, so innocent, so precious, so deserving of love and protection and all the things that a good parent provided. She would be that good parent, Cara vowed. No matter what anyone else thought or said or believed, she would give her son everything she had never had, things that even his father had not enjoyed.

Somehow.

She settled down to wait for morning, one *ka-shunk* at a time.

Holt stretched, then sat up in the bed in his sister's room, the one in which Cara Jane might have slept if she hadn't been too proud or too wary or something. Thoughts of her had intruded far into the wee hours of the first morning of the new year, he realized as he swung his feet down onto the floor and stood. He had been too tired after the party to drive out to his ranch, and since Cara hadn't wanted to use this room, he'd figured he might as well.

While pulling on his clothes, he smelled bacon cooking. Hap—or someone—was making breakfast. Holt wondered if they had enough eggs in the house. He felt like he could eat a good dozen himself, despite the dinner and all the goodies he'd consumed last night. Bless Marie Waller anyway.

The pastor's wife had done her best to make up for Charlotte's absence these past weeks, sending over one dish or another with her husband, Grover, whenever he came to play at Hap's domino table, which was almost daily. Unfortunately, Grover suffered from diabetes, so those tidbits rarely included anything sweet, and Holt possessed a powerful sweet tooth. Maybe they'd get pancakes for breakfast if *someone* happened to be in the kitchen.

Hap happened to be in the kitchen, and by the time Holt got there, he'd burned the bacon.

"Does that look too done to you?" he asked, shoving the plate beneath Holt's nose.

"We've gotta get your glasses checked," Holt told him, taking the plate and sliding it onto the counter.

Hap grunted and handed over the spatula. "I reckon you better try your hand at the eggs this morning, then."

"You don't suppose the Garden's open, do you?" Holt asked glumly, referring to the café downtown.

Hap shook his head. "We could always ask Cara Jane to help out."

Sighing, Holt went to the refrigerator. "I don't know about her. Something's just not right there."

"She lost her man. All alone in the world with a boy to raise. That's what's not right."

"We don't know that," Holt grumbled, taking the egg carton from the refrigerator. "Why, for all we know, she isn't even that kid's mother."

"Have you looked at that child?" Hap scoffed. "If she's not his mama, then she's real close kin."

Holt had to admit that they favored each other. "Could be she's hiding out."

"From who? Not the law. That I won't believe."

Okay, she didn't strike Holt as a hardened criminal, either, but something about her didn't ring true. For one thing, he reasoned silently, a woman like her attracted men like honey attracted flies. If she'd hung tight back in Oregon, some fellow would have stepped up to take care of her and little Ace quick enough. Even if she'd loved her husband to distraction—and somehow he didn't think that had been the case—it didn't make a lick of sense for her to strike out on her own looking for someplace "happier."

"How do we even know she's widowed?" he asked, taking down a bowl to crack the eggs into. He preferred his eggs over-easy but that didn't mean he could cook them that way. Better to just scramble them and have it done with.

Hap considered, then shook his head. "I know that look too well. 'Sides, why lie about it? There's no law against leaving a husband. Even if she's scared of him, wouldn't it make more sense for her just to tell us that?"

"You mean, if he was abusive or something."

"Exactly."

Holt pulled open a drawer and took out a fork. "For all we know, she was never even married."

Hap humphed at that. "Don't strike me as that sort."

"Maybe not, but that would explain why she's not living off her husband's Social Security somewhere. It just doesn't add up. She hasn't been completely honest with us."

"No reason she should be, I reckon," Hap said, hobbling into the other room. "Maybe once she gets to trust us."

It seemed to Holt that his grandfather had that backward. How were they supposed to trust her if she didn't level with them about herself and her situation?

He cracked half a dozen more eggs and then took a certain pleasure in going after them with the fork.

Cara tapped on the window, her breath fogging the glass. Wearing the same clothes as he had the day before, Holt looked up from beating something in a bowl and reached out with one hand to flick open the door. His hair stuck up in disarray, and he needed a shave. Somehow that made him all the more attractive.

"'Morning," she muttered, sliding into the narrow room sideways, Ace on her hip. The dark shadow of Holt's beard glinted reddish-gold up close, she noticed.

"Happy New Year."

"Oh. Yes. Happy New Year."

"Sleep okay?"

"Just fine, thank you," she lied. As if he knew that her conscience pinched her, Ace patted her chest before grabbing a fistful of the front of her aqua-blue T-shirt. "Except," she amended, "I keep hearing a giant clock in the distance."

Holt turned to lean a hip against the counter. "A giant clock?"

"Well, not tick-tock, exactly. More like *ka-shunk, ka-shunk*."

Holt chuckled, folding his arms. "That's not a clock, giant or otherwise. It's a pump jack on an oil well out back."

She goggled at him. "Oil well! But wouldn't that make you rich?"

Holt flattened his mouth. "Hardly. And it doesn't belong to us. A previous owner kept the mineral rights to the property."

"Ah." That hardly seemed fair, but what did she know about it? To cover her ignorance, she smiled and asked, "How was the party?"

He went back to beating what she now recognized as a bowl full of eggs. "'Bout like you'd expect for a room full of old folks and a domino table."

Since she'd never had experience with either, she said nothing more about that. "Is your grandfather around?"

"He is. You and the boy wanting some breakfast?"

"No. No, thanks. We've eaten already." Crackers, applesauce and warm cheese sticks, but Holt didn't need to know that. "I can finish that up for you, though, if you want."

"If you're not eating, it wouldn't be fair to let you cook," he grumbled.

"I don't mind."

He jerked his head toward the doorway. "Hap's in the other room."

"Your choice," she mumbled, stung. So much for winning his favor.

Slipping by him, she carried Ace into the dining room. Hap sat with his head bent over a big black Bible. He looked up, smiling, and nodded at a chair. She sat down with Ace on her lap. She heard the clump of Holt's boots as he stepped into the doorway behind her.

Ignoring Holt, Cara said to his grandfather, "I'd like the job, Mr. Jefford."

"Well, now, that's fine." Hap gave his head a satisfied nod.

"There's just one thing," she went on, heart thundering. "I'd like for Ace and me to have our own place. If we could stay in one of the kitchenettes, that would be great."

While Hap scratched his neck, Holt spoke up. "What's wrong with Charlotte's room?"

"It's too small," she said bluntly, not looking at him. "Ace would have to sleep with me all the time." She addressed Hap again. "I could pay something, maybe half, so you wouldn't be out the whole rent."

To her relief, Holt walked back into the kitchen.

"No need for that," Hap said, reaching out to pat her hand. "'Course, if we're full up and need the space, you and Ace might have to move in here temporarily. That room of Charlotte's is a mite crowded, but I'm sure she'll take all her stuff when she and Ty get their house built."

He went on chatting for some time about the house that Charlotte and her husband, Tyler, were planning to build in Eden, while Cara floated on a wave of relief and delight. When Holt came in with two plates of scrambled eggs, burnt bacon and white bread, Cara smiled brightly. Employed and with a place of her own, she finally let herself believe that this might work out.

"I'll see to those black-eyed peas now," she said cheerfully, rising to her feet and sliding Ace onto her hip, "and clean up the kitchen once you're done here."

Hap chuckled. "It's a holiday. The cleaning can wait till later."

"Thank you, Mr. Jefford."

"Call me Hap. We're one big happy family here. Glad to count you in."

Smiling, Cara nodded and started to turn away, only to be brought back down to earth with a thud when Holt said matter-of-factly, "I'll be needing your ID and Social Security number." He forked up a big bite of eggs before pinning her with his gaze. "For the employment papers." She felt the color drain from her face, even though she'd expected this. He seemed not to notice, digging into his food. "You can give it to me after you get the peas on."

She nodded before making her escape.

One more lie, she told herself. Just one more, and then everything would be fine.

Chapter Four

Holt lifted the employment forms from the printer tray and placed it on the desk in front of Cara Jane. "That's the last one. At least I think so. These are all I use with my crew, and I don't see why this should be any different."

"Your crew?" she asked, busy filling in the blanks.

Ace played beneath the counter at her feet, crawling back and forth and screeching from time to time. As he answered her, Holt couldn't help smiling at the sounds of a little one at play. "Roughnecks. I run a crew of roughnecks. Two crews, actually, and three rigs."

"Oh." She kept her gaze trained on the tax form in front of her. "I remember you saying something about being a roughneck last night."

He suspected that she didn't have the faintest idea what a roughneck was. "I don't usually work as a motel maid," he told her drily. "I'm a wildcatter."

This time she did look up. "Wildcatter?"

He leaned forward slightly. "A driller. For oil."

Comprehension finally dawned. "Oh!"

Holt frowned. Wouldn't a girl who grew up in Oklahoma know *something* about the oil business?

Eyes narrowed, Holt pointed to the signature line. "Just sign here. Then I'll need a copy of your Social Security card and driver's license."

She signed on the appropriate line and pulled her wallet from the diaper bag at her feet.

"So you don't actually work for your grandfather at all," she said, handing over the laminated cards.

Holt inclined his head. "Just helping out since my sister married. Well, before that, really. Since they got engaged at Thanksgiving. They didn't marry until December seventh."

"That's not much of an engagement," Cara Jane commented wryly, pushing back the desk chair and leaning forward to reach for Ace.

"Two whole weeks," Holt supplied, carrying her license and Social Security cards to the scanner.

She straightened, pulling Ace up onto her lap. "Goodness. I was engaged for two years."

Holt punched a button and looked at her as she stood, swinging the boy onto her hip. "Didn't you say you married at eighteen?"

"That's right."

He gaped. "Your parents let you get engaged at *sixteen?*"

Her gaze met his briefly. "Let me? I doubt they even noticed." She poked the boy in the chest with one fingertip, saying, "Don't you go getting any ideas, dude. You're going to college before you get married, just like your daddy."

Holt latched onto that tidbit of information. "So your husband had a degree?"

She glanced at him, wary now, and Holt could see her trying to decide what to tell him. Finally, she said, "He was a lawyer."

A lawyer? Holt thought of those two lightweight suitcases

he'd carried into her room and the eight-year-old car from which he'd taken them. He put that together with her reaction and came up with...more questions.

"I thought lawyers usually made a pretty good living."

"So did I," she said.

Rubbing his prickly chin, Holt pondered this bit of information, remembering that she'd said her husband hadn't wanted her to work, even though they'd been married at least six years, by Holt's reckoning, before Ace's birth. Holt filed that away, allowing her to change the subject as he retrieved her identity documents.

"So," she said, a bit too brightly, as he handed them over, "you're not employed here, but I take it you live here."

"Here at the motel?" He shook his head. "Naw, I have a little place of my own, a ranch east of town."

"I see." Her expression changed not a whit, but relief literally radiated off her. "I guess that means you're, like, married."

Folding his arms, Holt asked, "Why would you think that?"

She lifted a shoulder, using both hands to anchor Ace on the opposite hip. "I don't know. Seemed like a reasonable conclusion for a man your age."

"What's my age got to do with anything? If you're thirty-six you must be married?"

"I didn't say that."

"Well, I'm not married," he told her, feeling rather indignant about her assumption, "which means I happen to be around here a lot. Every day, in fact."

She nodded at that, inching away. "Oh. I guess I'll be seeing you around then."

"Count on it," he told her, watching her snag the diaper bag then leave the room.

Even with the boy perched on her hip, she walked with a decidedly feminine stride. Holt shook his head, disgusted with himself.

A dead lawyer for a husband, engaged at sixteen, hadn't worked since high school, assumptions and secrets, and enticing, and he couldn't keep his gaze off her. Without a doubt, that woman was trouble walking. He just hadn't figured out exactly how yet. But he would. Oh, yes, he would.

Cara straightened, her arms full of rumpled linens, which she stuffed into the bag on the end of the cleaning cart. She took one more swipe at the newly made bed and hurried out to check on her napping son.

The backpack allowed her to tote him much of the time, but the thing became problematic when it came to certain chores, so she'd taken to hauling the crib from room to room with the cleaning cart. The portable baby bed resembled a playpen more closely than a conventional crib, anyway, and despite the cumbersome process, having her son within sight comforted Cara.

Unfortunately, she had no choice but to take the crib into the apartment at nap time and let Hap watch over Ace while he slept. Since Hap could routinely be found at the domino table in the other room, that usually necessitated little more than an open door between the apartment and the lobby, but Cara hated not being able to watch over Ace herself.

After locking the room, she pushed the cart across the pavement to the laundry, then moved on through the kitchen to the dining area. Her heart jumped up into her throat when she saw the empty crib. Then she heard a familiar squeal, followed by men's laughter, coming from the front room. She raced out into the lobby to find Ace sitting in the middle of the domino table, surrounded by chuckling old men, while he clutched handfuls of dominos.

"Look there, Hap," Justus teased. "He takes after you, hogging them bones."

"That's my boy." Hap patted Ace's foot.

"You wish," Teddy crowed.

"He's getting in practice for when Charlotte and Ty start their family," Grover Waller, the pastor, maintained. Round and cheerful, Grover reminded Cara of an aging, balding cherub in wire-rimmed glasses and clip-on tie, but at the moment all Cara could think was that these men had her son.

As she rushed toward them, Hap turned his head to grin at her, holding out an empty bottle. "He's had him a little snack, Mama, and a dry diaper."

"Took all three of us to change that boy's britches," Justus told her, sounding pleased.

"Strong as an ox," Teddy confirmed with a nod.

Cara began plucking dominoes from her son's grasp, her anxious heartbeat still speeding. "I apologize. This won't happen again. I—I'll pick up a baby monitor as soon as I'm paid, one I can carry around with me so I'll know the instant he awakes."

"No need, Cara Jane," Hap protested. "We don't mind watching out for him, do we, boys?"

"Not at all," Teddy said.

"Cheery little character," Grover put in.

"That's kind of you, but he's my responsibility," Cara said, gathering Ace into her arms. The relief she felt at simply holding him against her made the preceding panic seem all the more terrible. How could she have let him out of her sight for even a moment? Yet, she'd have to do the same thing repeatedly, for what other choice did she have?

Hap again patted Ace's foot, knocking his shoes together. "So long, little buddy."

Cara quickly carried her son from the room. She knew that she'd overreacted badly. Those old men meant no harm. They had no designs on her son. But Ace was her child, her responsibility, and she would give no one reason to question her ability to care for him.

Apparently her overreaction had been noted, for as she pushed the door closed, she heard Hap say, "She's mighty protective."

"Protective?" Justus scoffed. "You'd think we was trying to steal him."

"There's a story there," Grover murmured.

Carefully pushing the door closed, she laid her forehead against it. Ace tried to copy the motion, bumping her head with his. It didn't hurt, and he didn't fuss, but she soothed him with petting strokes anyway, sick at heart. Had she given them away? She shook her head. Impossible. These people had no idea who she really was. So they deemed her an overprotective mother. Let them think what they wished. Nothing mattered except keeping Ace safe and with her.

Except that they were bound to tell Holt how she'd reacted today, and that would be one more black mark against her in his book.

But she didn't have time to worry about Holt now. She had work to do. Sighing, she carried Ace out to the laundry room, got him into the backpack and returned to the apartment to fold up and move the portable crib.

One more room, and then dinner. And Holt.

He had not failed to show up for dinner the past two nights. On both occasions, he'd looked so weary that she'd have felt sorry for him if he hadn't watched her as though he expected her to pull a weapon and demand his wallet at any moment.

She held out the faint hope that he would have other plans for tonight, this being Friday. Didn't single men go out on the weekends in Eden, Oklahoma? Apparently not, because when she laid food on the table that evening, his big, booted feet were beneath it. As on the previous occasions, he barely spoke to her, just stared when he thought she wouldn't notice. She suffered through the meal in silence and hoped he would stay away the next time.

Not so. Even Hap expressed surprise when Holt arrived the next night. "It's not our usual Saturday night out," he exclaimed.

Holt brushed aside the old man's comments. "What of it? Still got to eat."

His brother Ryan arrived thirty seconds later. A big, bluff man with a good thirty pounds on Holt and dark, chestnut-brown hair and hazel eyes, Ryan greeted Cara with open delight.

"You are the answer to our prayers," he told her, holding her hand between both of his after their introduction.

Holt scowled and asked if Ryan would mind parking himself so they could eat. Ryan, who seemed to accept his role as younger brother with equanimity, sat. Hap prayed. Ryan then made friends with Ace, who occupied her lap as usual, while Holt scoffed down three pieces of grilled chicken and a truckload of macaroni and cheese before taking his leave again. At no point did he so much as speak to Cara, letting his nod suffice for both greeting and farewell.

Ryan, a very pleasant man, came into the kitchen later to sheepishly apologize for his brother. Cara pretended complete ignorance.

"I can't imagine why you'd think I'd be offended. I just work here."

"Work," Ryan said, "is a lot of the problem. You see, right now Holt's working too much. Well, he's always worked too much. It's just that now he's trying to catch up. My fault," he added with gentle self-deprecation. He then went on to explain that he had a hard time getting away from his responsibilities at the school, which had left Holt to take on the motel pretty much by himself. "Which is why I'm so delighted that you're here."

Cara didn't bother to point out that Holt obviously did not

share that delight. Instead, she thanked Ryan, finished the dishes, picked up Ace and slipped out quietly. She couldn't help thinking, though, that it wouldn't hurt Holt to be nicer to everyone, including his brother.

With Ryan turning out to be such a friendly man, much like Hap in that regard, Holt's surliness seemed all the more pronounced. It smarted that he didn't seem to like her, so much so that she intended to keep her distance on Sunday, her one full day off. On Sundays the Jeffords "closed the office." Sunday, Hap had told her, belonged to God, though they'd rent to anyone in need of a room who wandered by.

Ace actually let her sleep in a bit that morning. After feeding him breakfast and watching a church service on TV, she thumbed through a magazine and finally stepped outside. The weather had turned surprisingly warm. On impulse, she packed a lunch of sorts from her meager provisions, loaded Ace into the backpack and headed for the park.

Separated from the motel grounds by a stream that wound through the gently rolling landscape, the park had to be entered via a bridge adjacent to the downtown area some three blocks to the east. Along the way, Cara explored the town.

There wasn't much to Eden, as far as she could tell on foot: some houses built before the Second World War, some houses built after, and just a couple blocks of old brick storefronts on the main street, which happened to be named Garden Avenue. Absolutely everything stood closed, everything except, of course, for the inviting little white clapboard church on the corner of Mesquite Street, which ended right at the back of the motel. The church appeared to be doing box office business, judging by the number of cars that lined the street and surrounded the building.

The sign next to the sidewalk identified it as the First Church of Eden and named Grover Waller as the pastor. The place had such a warm, inviting air, much like Grover himself, that Cara took note of the service times. Perhaps she and Ace would visit there next Sunday. Since she assumed that the Jeffords attended there, given their close association with the pastor, it might even win her some points. But not with Holt.

She'd learned the hard way how impossible it could be to win the regard of someone who had made up his or her mind not to like her. Her in-laws had hated her on sight, but Cara had tried to win their regard, nonetheless, without success.

Putting the little church behind her, she took Ace to the park, where they ate their lunch in solitary peace and sharp winter sunshine.

Holt paced the floor in front of the reception desk that next Saturday night. Cara had never seen him dressed to go out. He "cleaned up good," as Hap put it. Wearing shiny brown boots, dark jeans with stiff creases, a wide leather belt, open-collared white Western shirt and a similarly styled brown leather jacket with a tall-crowned brown felt hat, he looked like the epitome of the Western gentleman. All cowboy. All man. He'd gotten himself a haircut, too, which gave him a decidedly tailored air but did nothing whatsoever to blunt his impatience.

"You really don't have to wait," she said again, bouncing Ace on her knee. "It's been almost two weeks. I can manage the desk until Ryan gets here."

In truth, she didn't expect to have to manage anything. The motel stayed full, or nearly so, during the week, but few guests strayed in during the weekends.

The last weekend had yielded only two rental opportunities, an older couple on their way up to visit relatives in Nebraska and a very young couple obviously looking for privacy. Hap had kindly but firmly turned away the last pair, saying only that he couldn't help them. Cara had learned a valuable lesson on how to handle an awkward situation that day.

"He should have been here already," Holt groused.

Cara opened her mouth to say that she was sure Ryan would be along soon, but just then, through the plate glass window, Cara spotted a now familiar late-model domestic sedan slow and turn off the highway into the lot. "There he is."

Holt spun to the window, bringing his hands to his waist. "It's about time." Striding to the end of the counter, he called through the open apartment door, "Granddad! He's here!"

"Comin'!" Hap called back, muttering, "Hold your horses. Always chomping at the bit."

Cara ducked her head, biting back a grin. Hap Jefford had quickly endeared himself to her and her son. Witty, caring and cheerful, he seemed genuinely fond of Ace and had even taken over much of the laundry chores once he decided that Cara had "got the hang of things," as he'd put it. If not for Holt coming around to glower at her, she thought she'd be fairly content. She'd tried to be nice to Holt, but that only made him more dour.

"Now, listen," Holt lectured, splaying a hand against the countertop.

"Isssssn!" Ace mimicked, leaning forward to smack his hand onto the lower counter.

Holt looked at him, one corner of his mouth kicking up. He glanced at Cara, sobered and cleared his throat, drawing back his hand. "Just let Ryan handle things. If anyone comes in, he'll take care of them. You're still observing for now."

"Hap's already explained," she began, only to have him cut her off.

"If you need anything, you have our numbers." He made a face. "Well, mine, anyway. Granddad never carries his phone with him."

"Why should I?" Hap asked, limping through the apartment door. "I never go anywhere on my own."

"On your own what?" Ryan asked, stepping inside the lobby.

"On my own by myself," Hap said. "How you doing, Ryan?"

"Excellent, as usual."

Holt rounded on his brother. "You took your time getting here."

Ryan paused in the act of shrugging off his corduroy coat and glanced at his wristwatch. "It's ten minutes till six. What's the rush?"

"Oh, don't mind him," Hap counseled, limping over to ruffle Ace's hair. "He's got a burr in his bonnet. I say, a burr in his bonnet." Ace giggled and fell back against Cara's chest. She smiled up at Hap, who patted her shoulder affectionately. "There's pizzas in the freezer, and if you eat them I won't be tempted."

"Done," Ryan proclaimed, rubbing his hands together.

"Can we go?" Holt demanded. "I'm hungry."

"When was the last time you *weren't* hungry?" Hap asked, limping around the counter.

"I'm usually pretty good when I get up from the table," Holt grumbled as the two of them left the building through the front door.

Ryan shook his head. "That's our Holt, two hollow legs."

"Not to mention a hollow head," Cara muttered.

Ryan burst out laughing. "I'm beginning to wonder if that's not his problem, though I've never thought so before." He stood staring as if that ought to make some special sense to her, then he clapped his hands together. "I'm thinking we should dress up those pizzas. What have you got in the pantry?"

"Pineapple?" she suggested hopefully.

"Pineapple?" he parroted. "They eat pineapple on their pizza up in Oregon? Sounds like a California thing. You ever get down to California?"

Cara just smiled, but inwardly she cringed. When would she learn to watch her mouth? The jangle of the telephone saved her from any more uncomfortable questions and the lies she'd rather not have to tell in answer. Ryan reached across the counter and picked up the receiver.

"Heavenly Arms Motel." He threw back his head and laughed. "Charlotte! How you doing, sugar? How's Ty and the Aldriches?"

Cara rolled the desk chair back, giving brother and sister as much privacy as possible. She tried not to listen, even considered slipping out of the room, but Ryan stood there, leaning on the counter and looking right at her as if she were as much a part of the conversation as he and his sister. He smiled and chatted, enjoying himself.

Finally he said, "I love you, too, sugar. We all miss you like crazy, especially Holt, I think. Y'all coming for the big game, then? Excellent. Looking forward to it. My best to Ty."

He hung up, beaming. "Get this," he said. "My brother-in-law usually attends the Super Bowl live. This year, he's passing it up and bringing Charlotte home to watch the game on TV with the family." He shook his head. "Now that's true love."

"You really care for her, don't you?" she said to Ryan.

He chuckled and spread his hands. "Of course. She's my baby sister. I'm told you have a brother, and I'm sure he loves you, too. That's just how it is."

Like Ryan, she had once thought that Eddie must naturally care for her, but all she had ever been to him was a conduit to the Elmont money.

"You and your brother and sister seem to have a special bond."

"Yeah." Ryan nodded, smiling to himself. "I guess, after our parents died, we sort of banded together, you know?"

She wasn't sure she did, really. Cara and her brother had, for all intents and purposes, raised themselves. Usually Eddie had gone his way and she had quietly gone hers. They'd had little in common, except for Addison, who'd been buddies with Eddie in high school.

Something Ryan had said suddenly struck her. "Did you say parents, as in plural? I was only told about your father's death."

Ryan passed a hand over his eyes and rubbed his cheekbone. Leaning both forearms on the counter, he drew a little closer and related the tale. "Yeah, Dad's death was a big shocker. You probably heard that he fell?" At her nod, Ryan went on softly. "Well, when our mother found out, she committed suicide."

Cara caught her breath. "Oh, I'm so sorry. I had no idea." Thinking of the moment she'd received news of Addison's death, she recalled the shock and the numbness, the uncertainty and the very great sadness. Part of that sadness, though, had been because she'd known she wouldn't really miss *him*, only the idea of raising their son together. "Your mother must have loved your father very much," she mused absently.

Ryan drew back at that. "I guess she did," he said, "but it marked Charlotte." He shrugged, adding, "Holt and I were already out of the house, young men. Charlotte was just thirteen and still at home, and she's never understood why Mom didn't think of her before she swallowed those pills."

Pills, Cara thought. She had more in common with Charlotte Jefford Aldrich than she'd realized. Neither of their mothers had cared enough about them to leave the pills alone. The knowledge saddened Cara and made her feel more kindly toward Charlotte.

Ace bucked and tried to slide off her lap, but she caught him up, hugging him tight. She loved him enough to put him first, and she always would. Thanks to the Jeffords, she now had a chance to establish herself as a fit guardian for him. If the Elmonts came calling, they would find no reason to again question her ability to care for her own son.

"That's why we're so happy God brought Ty and Charlotte together," Ryan said, "Next year, Ty wants to take all of us to the Super Bowl. Man, wouldn't that be something!" He shook his head. "Not that it'll happen, mind you."

"What makes you say that?" Cara asked. From what she'd seen and heard, Tyler Aldrich appeared to be a very generous and wealthy man, with the kind of money that even the Elmonts must bow to. If he wanted to take his in-laws to the Super Bowl, what was to stop him?

Ryan tapped a thumb on the countertop and considered. "You're right! You're here. You'll be an old hand at this by then. Why shouldn't we all go if we want to?"

Cara smiled. At least one of the Jefford brothers had confidence in her. Too bad it wasn't Holt. Irritated with herself, she tried to put him out of her mind. Why his approval continued to mean so much to her, anyway, she couldn't imagine. Besides, Ryan clearly had just as much influence with their grandfather as Holt did.

Determined that she would not subject herself to Holt's disapproval, Cara excused herself a couple hours later when his dirty, white double-cab pickup truck appeared in the frame of the picture window overlooking the highway. A sleeping Ace in her arms, she said good-night to Ryan, left him to deal with the leftover pizza and slipped through the apartment and out the back.

She couldn't help feeling a little sorry for herself as she cradled her son in one arm and let herself into the dark, silent room. Despite her gratitude for the sanctuary she'd found here in Eden, it hurt to know that no one else in the world cared about her, not her brother, certainly not her in-laws.

At first Cara had thought being married would fill that void in her. Eventually, however, she'd realized that Addison really valued only one thing about her, that he could control her. She'd been his outlet for the control that his parents had exerted over him and his sister. That had been her sole function in his life.

When she'd at last been granted a child, she'd believed that things could change between her and her husband. Then Addison had died, and his parents had plotted to cut her out of her son's life altogether. To top that off, her own brother had been willing to help them, for a price, because that's all she'd ever been to him, a means to an end, a way to stay close to Addison, who would have dropped Eddie long ago if not for her.

The only person to ever really love Cara had been her great-aunt. Cara still missed her aunt deeply, and with tears in her eyes, she vowed to honor her aunt's memory by giving her son all that the *real* Cara Jane Wynne had given her, and at least one other thing that Aunt Jane had never thought or intended to share.

Her name.

Chapter Five

Holt guided his truck to a stop beneath the motel drive-through behind Ryan's sedan and killed the engine. Hap sent him a sharp glance, then grinned when Holt opened his door and stepped one foot down to the ground.

"I take it you're coming in."

"Well, of course I'm coming in."

"You don't always."

"So?"

Hap just shook his head and slid out on his side.

Why shouldn't he come in? Holt asked himself. He didn't always go haring off back to the ranch after dinner, and no one could say he did. Grumbling at the strange behavior of some folks lately, Holt strode ahead of his grandfather up the sloping walkway and into the building.

The TV played in a room lit only by it, a lamp and the glowing embers revealed by the open door of the potbellied stove. A replica of an 1890s model, the stove provided the cheery ambience of a crackling fire with less hassle and more actual heat than a fireplace. Ryan looked up from his customary spot on the sofa.

"Hey. Charlotte called. She and Ty are coming home for Super Bowl Sunday."

"That's good!" Hap crowed, hobbling past Holt on his way to his favorite rocking chair.

"Where's Cara Jane?" Holt wanted to know, ignoring the fact that his brother-in-law would give up a live Super Bowl game in order to bring Charlotte back home for a visit. Matters here seemed more important at the moment. If Cara Jane had waltzed out and left Ryan on his own to watch over things, Holt would be having a talk with her.

"She just took Ace back to their room," Ryan told him off-handedly.

Strangely deflated, Holt craned his neck. The thing seemed to have more kinks than a flattened bedspring tonight. "Why'd she do that? Some reason she didn't want to say good-night?"

Ryan sent him a blank look. "Don't think so. She'd rocked Ace to sleep and was just waiting for you two to show up so she could put him down for the night."

"Oh." Holt turned to stare blindly at the television set, trying to appear relaxed and unconcerned. "So, how'd it go?"

Ryan kicked back on the sofa, crossing his hands behind his head. "Quiet. Real quiet. And I don't mean just businesswise. She's not much for conversation, is she? I mean, we talked some, but it's not like she really says anything, not about herself, anyway." He grinned at Holt. "Fortunately, I'm able to carry a conversation all on my own. The two of you would probably bore each other to tears, though, given how little you each have to say."

Holt grunted at that. He didn't think of Cara Jane, or himself, as boring. Quiet, yes, but boring? No way.

"I'm a little concerned about her, though," Ryan went on.

Holt's attention perked up. "How so?"

Ryan looked to Hap. "She seemed, I don't know, sad. And

doesn't she strike you as awful thin? I think she's lost weight since she's been here. The girl's no bigger than a child to begin with. Seems like a lonely little thing, too, despite the way she dotes on that boy. I don't think he got off her lap the whole evening."

Hap nodded. "She don't hardly give you a chance to get to know Ace or for him to get to know you. I could lighten her load a whole bunch just by watching over him sometimes, but she won't hear of it 'less he's napping." Hap shook his head worriedly. "I'm wondering how long she can hold up."

Ryan looked to Holt. "Maybe you and I ought to be taking a bit more of a hand, still."

Perversely, Holt had to bite his tongue to keep from telling Ryan to just back off and leave Cara Jane to him. He knew it wasn't reasonable and that rankled. He'd already had a talk with himself and God about his attitude toward Charlotte, and he didn't want to have to add Ryan to that list. He still couldn't believe what a load his baby sister had carried all those years, and God knew Holt wanted her happiness above even his own, but he couldn't deny that he'd felt a twinge of resentment at having to put his own work on hold in order to take care of what had been hers. Now, suddenly, he wanted to snap at his brother. And why? He knew the answer to that, and it had a lot less to do with Ryan than Cara Jane.

Narrowing his eyes, Holt wondered what she had been up to here on her own with his brother. Had she played on Ryan's sympathies? Maybe even tried to spark his interest? Ryan would be too trusting, too soft-hearted to properly judge the situation. He wouldn't understand how Holt could be so sure that Cara Jane wasn't being completely honest with them. Nope, this burden fell to him. So be it.

"I think I'll just check on things before I shove off," Holt announced, striding for the apartment door.

"You sure that's a good idea?" Ryan asked.

"I'll see the two of you later," Holt answered, as if he hadn't even heard the question.

"The boy was sleeping," Ryan began, but Hap cut him off, calling out a cheery, "Tell Cara Jane good night for me."

Holt kept on walking, right into the apartment and out the back door. He dashed across the pavement to her room, cold nipping at his ears and nose. If Cara Jane Wynne had designs on his too-trusting and too-amiable brother, Holt felt an obligation to find out and put a stop to it.

Of course, he'd felt the same way about Ty when he'd first realized that he and Charlotte might be interested in each other. Holt had feared that, with wealth almost beyond imagining, Tyler might consider Charlotte as nothing more than another plaything. In the end, Ty had turned out to be madly in love with Charlotte and willing to give up his whole world, family and career included, to make her happy. She'd refused to allow him to make that sacrifice. Thankfully, neither had to give up anything for the other. As it turned out, Ty would continue to run Aldrich & Associates even after he and Charlotte built their house and moved to Eden, and to everyone's surprise, the snooty Aldrich clan had accepted Charlotte with open arms.

Cara Jane, however, was nothing like Tyler Aldrich. Holt wanted to be fair, but whenever he came into contact with her, his every sense jolted to uneasy alert. He sensed that desperation hid beneath her quiet aloofness, and it made Holt wonder what secrets she held and to what lengths she might go to keep them hidden.

He stood in front of her door now, his hand fisted, but instead of knocking, he closed his eyes and reached for help, preparing himself for the encounter.

Father, You know I don't trust this girl, and I know that I tend to react in defensive anger to anyone who threatens my family. That serves no useful purpose for anyone. Help me here. I don't want to be unkind or harsh. I just want to protect my family and myself.

Himself?

Holt's eyelids snapped open. Yes, himself. All wrapped up in that small package lived a very pretty and compelling woman who made him aware of her as none other ever had. She took him back to a time when he'd thought he would marry and have a family of his own—until his daddy had died.

He'd taken up where his dad had left off, even hiring some of his father's old crew, and he'd accepted that God did not intend for him to marry and make a family of his own. Over the years, Holt had seen too many men crippled, broken down and even killed working on oil rigs. Sure, the odds had improved, but the chances of an accident were still too great. Besides, his brother, sister and grandfather needed him.

In all fairness, Cara Jane could not be faulted for making him think of a time when his life had seemed destined for a different path. He sucked in a deep breath of cold air and finished his prayer.

Help me be fair and insightful, Lord. Give me discernment so I'll know how best to deal with Cara Jane. Accomplish Your will in this and protect my family. Amen.

Calmly he lifted his hand and tapped on the door, mindful of the boy sleeping within. Seconds later he felt Cara Jane standing just behind that barrier. Backing up a step, he lifted his chin so his face wouldn't be hidden by the brim of his hat and she could see him clearly through the peephole. The chain snicked, and then the door opened a few inches.

Head bowed, she regarded him warily from beneath her brows. "Something wrong?" She sounded stopped-up, and he wondered if she might be getting a cold.

"I don't know," he answered. "You tell me. But do it

inside, please. It's freezing out here." He bounced his shoulders up and down beneath his leather coat to emphasize that fact. She had to be chilly, too, standing there in nothing more than jeans and a tank top. Didn't the woman own anything with sleeves?

She turned away from the door, and he pushed inside, glancing around.

"Where's Ace?"

Cara Jane sent a fleeting, twisted smile over one shoulder. "In his room."

"What room?"

She moved toward the closet, crooking a finger at him. Basically, one passed through the closet area to the bath beyond, which could be closed off with louvered doors for privacy. She'd hung a blanket over the outer, open doorway into the closet and now pulled it aside. Puzzled, Holt walked across the floor to look behind the blanket.

The closet provided ample space for the small crib, especially since no clothing hung from the single rod overhead. The louvered doors that separated the bath area from the closet and the foot or so of space at the bottom of the blanket provided ample ventilation. The pebbled glass of the high window in the bathroom would filter sunshine into the space in the daytime, and the light in the toilet cell made a decent night-light.

Ace slept deeply in this makeshift nursery, a soft bundle of baby boy at complete peace with his little world. Holt's heart turned over in his chest. His mother might not be trustworthy, but Ace deserved only protection and consideration.

Backing out of the space, Holt took a look around and noted all the little ways in which Cara Jane had made this space a home for herself and her son, from the sprig of ivy falling over the lip of a water glass to the dish towel folded and fanned prettily across the bar counter. She'd fashioned a seat for Ace at the breakfast bar from an upturned cooking pot, a pillow and a woven belt arranged on a dining chair.

"Looks like you've settled in nicely," he commented, keeping his voice low.

Nodding, Cara Jane floated about the room and came to rest with her hands gripping the back of the dining chair she'd obviously chosen for her own.

"What's going on?" she asked.

Holt watched her study the hard wood seat of the chair. After a moment, he realized that she had yet to look him in the eye. She sniffed and made a swipe at one cheek, and suddenly he knew why she hadn't looked at him. He wandered over to the hide-a-bed sofa and sat down, just so she'd know that he meant to stay awhile. He removed his hat and turned it over in his hands.

Deciding that a direct approach would serve best, he asked, "Why are you crying?"

She shot him a wary look, moved around the chair and gingerly parked herself. "I don't know. Women cry sometimes."

He leaned back and crossed his legs, leaving the hat on his lap. "Last time Charlotte cried," he told her, "it was over Ty."

Cara Jane didn't appear to muster much interest in that, but she politely replied, "Oh?"

"Mmm-hmm. Never thought she'd see him again, I guess. That's when I started praying especially hard."

"And now they're married," Cara Jane said, a touch of asperity, or possibly envy, in her voice.

"Happily married," he confirmed.

Cara Jane gripped the seat of her chair with both hands. "Charlotte's very lucky. You all are." Spearing him with a tart look, she added, "Oh, that's right. You don't believe in luck."

"We're blessed," he admitted, tickled for some reason by her irritation, "and we know it."

"Do you? Even after the way your parents died?" He must have shown his surprise at that because she quickly added in an apologetic tone, "Ryan told me about your mother."

"I see." Obviously Ryan had more than carried his end of the conversation.

For a long moment, she said nothing, just sat there looking down at her hands, the palms turned up as if weighing the words she might speak. Her irritation gave way to wistfulness as she said, "It's odd, isn't it? Your dad fell to his death. My husband fell. Your mom took pills. My mom took pills." As if fearing she'd said too much, Cara Jane quickly tucked her hands beneath her thighs. "Not on purpose," she qualified. "My mom just liked to get high. She liked it so much it killed her."

Holt should have been pleased to learn something new about her, but instead he wished she hadn't told him, wished it hadn't happened in the first place, wished it didn't make him feel sorry for her. He especially wished he didn't have to know more, but he did.

"How old were you?"

"Seventeen."

Old enough to stay out of the child welfare system, he noted, not old enough to really take care of herself. A heaviness settled over him. He accepted it with the gravity it deserved, asking, "What about your dad?"

She waved a hand. "Last we heard he was living on the streets up in Vancouver, but for all I know, he could be anywhere. That was ten, twelve years ago."

No wonder she'd married so young. Mother dead of a drug overdose, father gone. This information put Cara Jane in a somewhat new light. Holt acknowledged reluctantly to himself that he'd asked for understanding and God seemed to be delivering it bit by bit.

With an inward sigh, he commented, "Sounds like you had it pretty rough growing up."

Cara Jane nodded. After a moment, she confessed, "I loved school. I was safe there."

Meaning she hadn't been safe at home. Holt inhaled through his nostrils. "What about the summers?"

"My mother's aunt," Cara Jane answered instantly. "I don't think either me or my brother could have survived without her." Her lips curved wistfully.

"Where's your aunt now?"

The shutters came down behind her eyes, and she shifted on her seat. "Great-aunt," she corrected, "and she died a long time ago."

"What about your brother?" Holt probed, but apparently she'd reached the limit of her willingness to share because she stood then and moved to the door.

"My brother and I are not close. We're not all so lucky—" She broke off, ruefully bowing her head. "Blessed, I mean. We're not all so blessed as you and Ryan and Charlotte." She leaned back against the door frame and folded her arms, blatantly changing the subject then. "Did Hap enjoy his night out? I imagine you're both pretty tired by now."

Holt knew when he was being asked to leave. He got to his feet and walked toward her, his hat in his hands. "Hap always enjoys his night out," he told her. "Guess it's your turn next."

"My turn?"

He hadn't intended this, but suddenly it seemed like a very good idea. He'd learned something about her tonight. What might he learn given a little time with her in a purely social setting?

"If Charlotte were here, it would be her turn," he pointed out, "but since she's not and you are…" He let that trail off, pressing lightly, "You're not going to make me go to dinner next week by myself, are you? No fun in that."

Cara Jane lifted her chin. "But I have Ace."

"Bring him along," Holt told her, reaching around her for the door knob. She leapt out of the way, and he pulled the door open. "It'll be a night out for both of you." With that, he stepped onto the pavement and pulled the door closed behind him, giving her no chance to refuse.

Only then did it occur to him that he'd just usurped her Saturday evening off. But for a good cause, he told himself, an essential cause. Not only did he need to learn more about her, Ryan was right. She had lost weight. She didn't fill out those jeans quite as well as when she'd first arrived, and if he hadn't been trying so hard not to pay attention, he'd have noticed it sooner. This working herself to the bone had to stop, which meant that he would have to step in once more. Perhaps he could see her well fed while he pumped her for information.

Holt fitted his hat onto his head as he strode over to the apartment and let himself in through the kitchen.

He found Hap and Ryan at the dining table, eating leftover pizza. Hap dropped his piece when Holt blew into the room.

"Caught ya. You know you're not supposed to be eating that. Too much sodium."

Hap made a face. "You won't tell Charlotte, will you?"

Holt circled around to his usual chair and dropped down into it, snatching the pizza off Hap's plate on the way. "Nothing to tell," he said, cramming the first bite into his mouth. Pineapple. That was new. Not half-bad, either.

"Not now that you've eaten it yourself," Hap groused, and Holt grinned.

"You're in a better mood," Ryan noted, claiming a second piece for himself. "Guess Cara Jane's okay."

Holt shook his head. "Nope. You're right. Work's too much for her."

Hap sighed and sat back in his chair. "What're we gonna do? I'm telling you now, I'm not putting her and Ace out on the street."

"No one's suggesting that," Holt said, though he might have if she hadn't opened up just a bit. It hit him that she hadn't ever really said why she'd been crying, which made for one more mystery. "We don't have any choice except to pitch in until we can find her some part-time help."

"But we've already tried that," Ryan pointed out. "We couldn't find anyone to hire, and I couldn't free myself up enough to make any difference."

"Let me rephrase," Holt said, downing the last of Hap's pizza. He reached for the one remaining piece. "*I* will just have to pitch in until we either find her some help or she loosens her grip on the boy."

Hap rubbed his chin. "If you could just help her after he gets up from his nap, say around three in the afternoon…"

Holt shrugged. "I guess I can manage that."

"And I'll be doing the dinner dishes from now on," Hap vowed, nodding his approval.

"No, I will," Ryan said, "and that includes the weekends, especially Sundays."

"Now how are you gonna manage—"

Ryan cut off Hap's protest with a raised hand. "I'll figure it out. It's only fair."

Hap looked at Holt, who shrugged again. Couldn't argue with fair.

"Speaking of Sundays," Hap said to Holt. "You invite her to go with us to church tomorrow?"

Holt made a face. "No, I didn't."

"I'll do it on my way out," Ryan volunteered, half rising from his chair.

"It can wait till morning," Holt insisted, focusing on his

pizza. "She, um, looked like she'd be turning in when I left, so I'll ask her in the morning."

Ryan subsided, but Holt caught the look he traded with Hap. He started to protest, but then he thought better of it. Letting Ryan think he had personal interest in Cara Jane would be one way of protecting Ryan. Cara Jane could not be described as an open book yet, and until he knew a lot more about her, Holt decided, it seemed best for everyone concerned to keep her out of Ryan's way.

He didn't want to think about why that especially seemed best for him.

Instead, he bit off another chunk of pizza. The sweetness of the pineapple provided a nice counterbalance to the spicy pepperoni. "Where'd you come up with this?" he asked Ryan, knowing his brother's penchant for dressing up a frozen pie.

"I didn't. That was Cara Jane's idea. West Coast influence, I suppose."

West Coast? Holt asked himself. Definitely not the Pacific Northwest. He'd expect fish pizza from that part of the world, not tropical additions.

Questions and answers and more questions. Well, he'd never expected it to be simple with that woman, not from the moment he'd first laid eyes on her.

Dinner next week should prove interesting. Very interesting.

Chapter Six

Cara glanced at the door, a spoon poised to fill Ace's gaping mouth with a grayish glob of cereal. A second flurry of knocks had her inserting the cereal into Ace's mouth at the same time as she called out, "Coming!"

Rising from the breakfast bar, she reached over to shut off the television as she hurried to answer the knock. She liked to hear the hymns that played early on Sunday mornings. Slipping the chain, she opened the door. Hap and Ryan stood smiling at her.

"Mornin', sunshine!" Hap greeted her. "We heard the TV and figured you was up."

She started to smooth her hands down her cotton print bathrobe, realized that she still held the spoon and dropped her hands to her sides instead. "We're having breakfast."

"Won't keep you then," Hap said, adding with a wag of his thumb, "Ryan and me, we was hoping you and Ace might like to join us for church this morning."

"You already know the pastor," Ryan pointed out.

"Grover Waller," she supplied, nodding. "First Church, right?"

"That would be the one," Hap confirmed.

"Actually, I was already planning to go there this morning. I saw the church building last week on our way to the park."

Hap literally beamed at that news.

"No need to go on your own," Ryan said. "Holt will be along in a few minutes with his truck, and there's room enough for all of us."

She made a face. The last person she needed to be spending time around was Holt. "Oh, but we'd have to switch out the car seat and all that," she said, thinking quickly. "We'll just meet you there. Easier that way."

"If you say so," Hap told her. "We'll try to save you a place, but don't be late."

She thanked them, said the appropriate goodbyes and closed the door. Ace smacked the tabletop with one hand and reached for the cereal bowl with the other. Even as she hurried over to finish feeding him, she wondered if she really should go to church today. She couldn't seem to keep her mouth shut around Holt, and the more he knew about her, the more likely he was to disapprove. Keeping her distance seemed the best course, but really, how much trouble could she get into attending a church service? Besides, she'd already agreed to go.

In all truth, she wanted to go. She couldn't help being curious and even a little hopeful about it in a way that she couldn't quite peg. Her only experience with church had come during those summers with Aunt Jane, but she'd always felt somewhat out of place in a congregation comprised mostly of elderly folk, and those services had been nothing like what she saw on television, which tended to leave her with more questions than answers. Knowing Grover, however slightly, and Hap and Ryan and Holt, she felt instinctively that the First Church would be different from anything she could imagine.

It seemed foolish not to satisfy her curiosity, which had

grown since she'd prayed for help just before she'd seen the
Help Wanted sign here at the Heavenly Arms. Seemed like the
least she could do after that was sit through a worship service,
even if she'd have to do it in short sleeves and with Holt breathing down her neck.

"You two have done enough," Holt complained, waving his
grandfather and brother toward the church door. "If you'd let
me handle it, I'd have convinced her to ride along with us."

"Bullied her, you mean," Ryan corrected with a grin.
"What's with you two, anyway?"

Holt ignored that last comment, making a sharp, slicing
motion with his hand. "Just go on and save us a seat. If you
can."

Where was the woman, anyway? As the others hurried into
the church, Holt turned back to stand sentinel on the sidewalk.

So Ryan wanted to know what was with the two of them,
did he? Only that Holt's every instinct told him Cara Jane had
secrets that were potentially harmful to him and his family.

With a grimace, he admitted to himself that it was more than
that. His head fairly buzzed every time he thought about her,
bringing up emotions that he'd believed long buried. No one
else needed to know these things, though. Once he'd uncovered her secrets, then he would decide whether or not to discuss
his concerns with anyone else. That seemed fair to everyone.
He wouldn't worry Hap and Ryan that way or cast undue suspicion on Cara Jane.

While scanning the area for her little car, his gaze snagged on
a small figure striding toward him on the other side of the street.
Correction. Two small figures, one carrying the other on her hip.
He'd know that sleek, pale, moon-gold hair anywhere. The dress,
however, caught him completely off guard. Putting a hand to the
crown of his hat, he clamped his jaw to keep it from dropping.

Beneath her usual denim jacket, she wore a swingy little flowered confection that flipped and swirled about her shapely knees in flashes of vibrant pinks, oranges and purples as she walked. Coupled with the jaunty bounce and flip of her shoulder-length hair, the effect was nothing short of mesmerizing.

As she drew closer, he saw that her toes were bared by sandals, purple sandals with high platform soles and ankle straps. How she'd walked all this way in those shoes, he couldn't imagine. Moreover, not a stitch of that outfit could be deemed appropriate for this gray, chilly weather. She had to be freezing her toes off, but my, what toes they were, dainty and shapely and breathtakingly female, like everything else about her.

She hurried toward him, Ace clutched against her side with both hands. Holt went to meet her, torn between shaking her and draping her with his coat. He settled for sliding an arm across her shoulders and a scold.

"What is wrong with you? Wearing *that* in this weather? I mean, isn't it pretty cool up in Oregon? Don't you have any warm clothes?"

She stopped and shrugged free of him, frowning. "Yes, it's cool up in Oregon." Tugging at the bottom of her jacket, she sniffed and turned her head away. "Maybe I'm impervious to the cold. Maybe I got so used to it up in chilly Oregon that I don't need such heavy clothing as you." She leaned sideways slightly and attempted to hitch Ace up a little higher on her hip while holding her skirt down at the same time.

Irritated as well as intrigued, Holt reached over and plucked the boy out of her grasp. He weighed more than Holt expected, too much for her to constantly carry around, and she clearly didn't like letting go of him, but Holt didn't particularly care at the moment. She had just lied to him through chattering teeth. But they didn't have time to discuss it now.

"If we don't get inside, we'll be standing through the service," he told her, not bothering to moderate his tone.

She clamped her teeth together, slashed a look at Ace and marched forward, arms swinging. Holt caught up in one long stride, unwilling to watch her walk away from him in that swishy skirt.

The opening strains of the gathering music reached his ears as they stepped up onto the broad stoop that fronted the building. At the same time, Ace reached up and grabbed the brim of his hat, tugging it down. Frowning disapproval at the boy, Holt removed the hat and used it to wave Cara Jane forward, his hand coming to rest in the small of her back as they pushed through the double doors into the church.

The place, as anticipated, was packed, and the congregation had already risen to sing the opening hymn. Ryan tossed them a wave from their usual pew up near the front of the building, but just then Agnes Dilberry scooted her brood down and made a place for them on the back row. Cara Jane reached up to take Ace into her own arms again, whispering that they would sit in the rear of the building so she could slip out in case he fussed. Holt didn't bother hissing back that she could always take Ace to the nursery in the other building. He already knew that she wouldn't let the kid out of her sight unless she had no other choice. Instead, he crowded into the pew next to her and accepted the open hymnal that Agnes passed to him, her eyes full of curiosity and speculation. Holt nodded his thanks.

Ace made a grab for the book and caught Holt by the wrist instead. Then the little fellow just sort of leaned and crawled his way right back into Holt's arms. Dismay flashed over Cara Jane's face, but Holt shifted the boy to his other arm to keep her from taking him back. Mama had to learn to let go sometime, and besides, the kid obviously liked him. Maybe she'd loosen her grip some after this.

She took the hymnal from him and held it open for them to share. He edged closer and resisted the urge to slide his arm around her. For one thing, he still held his hat in that hand, and one of the Dilberry scamps already eyed it covetously. For another, it surprised and alarmed him how natural the impulse felt. Befriending her until he knew that she posed no threat to his family was one thing; letting himself get caught up in something too personal for his own good would be nothing short of insanity.

Holt trained his focus straight ahead, the boy held tight in the crook of his arm, and tried not to think about how pretty she looked in that flowered dress with her pale hair flipping up against the tops of her slender shoulders and her dainty toes peeking out of those ridiculous shoes. She needed a good coat, he decided, preferably one that covered her from the top of her head right down to the ground.

Cara glanced around, surprised to find the church on the smallish side. The large, rectangular, flat-topped two-story brick annex in back made it feel like a larger place from the outside, but the inside told another story.

Constructed of pale wood from floor to ceiling, including the pews, the room felt somewhat bare, despite the many bodies crowding the unpadded pews. Only the bright, greenish-blue carpet covering the raised platform at the front of the building and the swirls of green, gold and blue glass in the tall narrow windows lent color to the space, while the crisp white altar, lectern and three armless chairs on the platform gave it a pristine feel. A brass cross stood upon the altar and before it sat a low, fresh arrangement of yellow carnations, white mums and ivy in a simple basket. Overhead hung airy fixtures of gleaming brass with tapered, frosted bulbs.

A young woman with light hair rolled into a tight knot at

the nape of her neck enthusiastically played the dark, upright piano to one side of the dais while a tall, thin, pale man followed along on an acoustic guitar. The voices of the congregation, including Holt's smoky baritone, literally filled the space to overflowing, much to her son's delight.

Ace bounced in the crook of Holt's elbow, waving his little arms as if directing the cacophony of notes. His blue eyes danced in time to the music. That alone made Cara smile. The man at her side did not.

She should have known that she couldn't escape Holt just by refusing a ride in his truck. Determined to ignore his high-handed manner and enjoy herself, Cara drank in every face, sound and gesture.

After the song, they sat for prayer, announcements and more music. An older couple warbled a duet to prerecorded accompaniment. Ace stood on the edge of the pew between Holt's legs, Holt's hands fastened securely about his waist, and jigged up and down to the tune, alternately clapping and laughing. At some point Holt had slipped off his leather jacket and draped it over the end of the pew. He tried to balance the hat on one thigh while wrangling Ace. Cara quickly realized that if she didn't rescue the hat, she'd surely have to buy him another. Ace seemed so happy that she didn't want to bother him. Instead, she tugged the hat into her lap, placing it crown down as Holt had done. Shortly thereafter, she traded the hat for her son as Ace threw himself sideways into her arms.

She knew a moment of extreme embarrassment when the offering plate came by a little later. First, she hadn't thought to bring so much as a nickle with her, and second, Ace latched on to the polished brass platter with feverish possession. While her face glowed hot and she tried to pry his little fingers from the rim, Ace squealed his baby delight and hung on for dear life, threatening to spill the contents onto the floor. Holt came to the rescue, plucking the plate from Ace's determined grasp with a chuckle and then Ace himself from her lap. Cara telegraphed her thanks with a wan smile. Holt just grinned and shook his head. She found that grin disconcerting. Somehow his frowns and glowers seemed easier to deal with.

They spent the remainder of the service passing boy and hat back and forth between them until the action became so mechanical that Cara barely noticed, her attention riveted by the sermon. Grover Waller turned out to be unlike any preacher Cara had ever heard. He didn't preach so much as converse, and the conversation did not proceed one-sided, either. Those in the congregation often spoke up with a hearty "Amen" or a simple answer to a question posed from the pulpit.

"So that we *know*," Grover said at one point, "that Christ went to the cross as a sacrifice for the sins of…who?"

"Me," said one fellow.

At the same time, someone else called out, "Everyone!"

A veritable chorus of "Amens" accompanied both. Nodding, Grover lifted his Bible and read from it.

"'He Who did not spare His own Son, but delivered Him up for us all, how will He not also with Him freely give us all things?'"

Grover went on reading, but Cara's mind had begun to whirl with so many unanswered questions that she didn't catch much more of it.

Finally, Grover finished up with, "'For I am convinced that neither death, nor life, nor angels, nor principalities, nor things present, nor things to come, nor powers, nor heights, nor depth, nor any other created thing, shall be able to separate us from the love of God, which is in Christ Jesus our Lord.'"

Cara leaned forward, trying to soak in what seemed to her to be a mountain of knowledge contained in this one sermon.

"Do you get this, brothers and sisters?" Grover asked,

laying down the Bible. "Nothing *created* can keep us from the love of God and the salvation that comes through His Son Jesus. What can then?"

"Sin," someone called.

"Our own unconfessed sin," Grover confirmed with a nod, "and our unbelief. Just that and nothing else."

Cara sat back with a *whump*. She believed, or at least she wanted to, but how could she believe in what she didn't really understand? And how could she confess what she must keep secret? She shook her head, so many questions crowding together inside of it, and felt the familiar weight of her son's hand on her cheek. Turning her head slightly, she puckered a kiss into his very sweaty little palm.

She realized suddenly that she should have peeled off a couple of his layers once they'd settled onto the pew, but she'd been so cold herself it hadn't occurred to her that Ace would quickly overheat in his warmer clothing. Practically shoving the hat at Holt, she pulled Ace onto her lap, but as soon as she began to tug off his outer layer, he started to buck in protest. It quickly became obvious that he would not give up even one layer without a fight. Exasperated, she did the only thing she could do. She stood and stepped over Holt's long legs into the aisle, heading for the exit.

Holt automatically drew his legs back when Cara Jane rose and stepped past him into the aisle. Only as she started for the door did he realize that she actually meant to leave the building, and only when she glared down at him did he realize that he'd reached out to stop her. Ace chose that moment to really kick up a fuss, squealing as he tried his best to squirm out of his mother's grasp. She made a dipping catch of Ace's suddenly eel-like body and surged forward, leaving Holt no option but to let go of her forearm. With heads turning from every direction, Cara Jane quickly slipped out of the building. Holt caught sight of Ryan's questioning gaze, shrugged and made his own escape as rapidly and unobtrusively as possible.

He paused on the broad stoop to cram his hat onto his head and toss on his coat. Cara Jane was already crossing the street when he stepped down onto the ground, but he loped off after her, surprised by how fast she could move with a squirming, howling Ace clasped to her chest. She'd covered half a block before Holt caught her.

"What's wrong with him?" he asked.

"He's overheated."

She kept walking, neither remonstrating with her son nor so much as glancing at Holt himself. He began to wonder why he'd come after her. Then he realized that her steps had begun to flag. When she heaved in a great breath of air, he reached out and snatched Ace out of her arms. Three things happened simultaneously: Ace shut up like a faucet turning off and reached up for the brim of Holt's hat, while Cara Jane stopped in her tracks.

Holt jerked his head back from Ace's questing fingers, coming to a standstill. This battle had to come sooner or later, he mused, might as well be now.

"Nope," he said firmly to the boy. Ace reached upward again. Holt shook his head, eluding those chubby but persistent hands. "No way, my man. Hat's off-limits." A third time he eluded capture of the hat brim by intercepting Ace in mid-grab. "Can't have the hat. No." Ace stared him in the eye for a moment, then crammed his hand into his mouth. Holt shifted around to face Cara Jane, dodging yet another attempt, this one somewhat wet. "No, and by the way, yuck."

Cara Jane hid a smile behind her hand. Once more Holt and Ace engaged in a mini staring contest. Finally Ace subsided with a sigh, his head sinking down onto Holt's shoulder. Triumphant, Holt addressed the boy's mother.

"I believe we have reached an understanding. I keep my hat, and he keeps his slime."

She threw out a nicely rounded hip and parked a hand on it, gray eyes sparkling. "Yeah? What's that rolling down the front of your jacket then?"

Holt looked down at the drool sliding down the front of his leather coat, at which point Ace reached up and neatly plucked the hat off his head by the brim. Proving too heavy for him, it promptly dropped to the ground. Chortling, Cara Jane lifted Ace from Holt's loose embrace and settled him onto her hip once more. Properly chastised, Holt swept up the hat and returned it to his head in one fluid movement, then pulled a handkerchief from his pocket and wiped the front of his coat clean. Falling into step beside Cara Jane, he wagged a finger at Ace.

"I've got your measure now, bud," he teased, "and you aren't to be trusted."

Ace grinned and lunged for him. Holt caught him with one arm and lifted off his hat with the other, while Cara Jane groaned, "Oh, brother. Here we go again."

"This time I'll trade you," Holt said. Holding Ace in the crook of his arm, he plopped the hat down on Cara Jane's head. She couldn't have looked more adorable if she'd tried.

"That's the trouble with babies," she said, rolling her eyes upward, "they pick up bad habits in a heartbeat."

Holt laughed. "Guess we did sort of set a standard back there, passing him back and forth like a sack of sugar."

She nodded and put her head down, the hat brim hiding her face from him. "You didn't have to follow us," she said. "I got him there, I can get him back on my own."

Holt shrugged. "The service was almost over anyway." He looked back, wondering how long before those doors opened and spilled people out. She shot him a wry, doubtful glance that made him say, "You're looking very pretty today. Cold, but pretty." Good grief, he was flirting with her, and now that he'd started he couldn't seem to find a way to stop. He eyed her head and quipped, "I especially like the hat. And the shoes."

She sputtered laughter, drawling, "Thanks. So glad you approve since someone told me they were inappropriate."

He hung his head at that. "Sorry. I didn't mean to snap earlier. It's just that I see you standing around shivering all the time in sleeveless tank tops and now sandals and I have to wonder why."

She sighed and reached up to sweep the hat from her head, holding it in front of her. "I know. I just didn't pack the right things before we set out. Goes to show you how tricky memories are. See, in my head, Oklahoma is this warm, golden place of warm, lazy days."

"The lazy, hazy days of summer," he commented.

She smiled dreamily. "Mmm, with the crickets making their music and the screen door slamming. I remember shadows dark as ink under the trees." She lazily waved one hand side to side, adding, "I can still feel the fan blowing back and forth, back and forth, filling the whole house with the smell of blackberry pie cooling on the kitchen table."

"Peach," he said, hugging his own memories close. "My grandma made the best peach pie in three counties."

"Ah, but the blackberries were free for the picking," Cara Jane reminded him. "We'd drive along the country roads and take what spilled over into the bar ditches."

"But the best thing about summer," he declared, nodding, "is watermelon."

"Ooooh. Ice-cold, juicy watermelon," she agreed. "I ate so much one time, I had juice dripping off my chin and running down my chest. I had to be rinsed off with a water hose before I could go back into the house."

"Well, of course. That's why you can't eat watermelon in the house," he teased. "You have to eat it sitting on the back porch so you can spit the seeds into the dirt between your bare feet."

She laughed at that. "I can just see it. You, Ryan and Hap—about thirty years younger—sitting on the edge of the porch, eating and spitting and covered in sticky watermelon juice."

"Don't forget old Chuck," Holt said, grinning. "He was the best spitter of the lot."

"And who is Chuck?"

Some of the joy of the moment dimmed. "My daddy," Holt told her. "Charles Holt Jefford, but everybody called him Chuck."

"You're named for him," Cara Jane remarked softly.

Holt nodded. "Partly. Holt for him, Michael for my mother's father, Michael Carl Ryan."

She lifted a finger. "I see a pattern developing."

Holt laughed. "You do, indeed. My brother is named Ryan Carl Jefford. Grandpa Mike died when we were little bitty, and Grandma Ryan way before that. Mama worshipped Grandpa Mike because it was just the two of them, and then she worshipped Daddy after Mike was gone."

Cara Jane nodded. "It's funny how much we have in common, isn't it? My husband's name was Charles, and he was named for his father. Plus, my mother's parents died before I was even born."

Frowning, Holt said, "I thought your husband's name was—"

"Addison Charles," she supplied. "That's where Ace comes from. A for Addison. C for Char—" She stopped dead in her tracks, and suddenly Holt knew he'd stumbled onto another of her secrets. A for Addison, C for Charles...

"And E? What's E stand for, Cara Jane?"

"Edward," she said angrily, though which of them she was angry at, Holt didn't know. "For my brother."

"I thought you weren't close to your brother."

"That's right."

"So you named your son after a brother you aren't even close to?"

"You can always hope, can't you?" she demanded, reaching for Ace.

Holt swung away. Ace huffed against his neck, and that's when he realized that the boy had fallen asleep. He spread his hand across that little back and looked down at Cara Jane, feeling warm and protective and chilled and suspicious all at the same time.

"I'll carry him," he muttered darkly, wishing that every moment with her didn't end up tainted by distrust and suspicion.

They walked in silence the rest of the way and parted at her door with whispered farewells. Sighing, Holt headed back to the church, the keys to the truck heavy in his pocket and misgivings heavy on his heart.

Chapter Seven

"Here it is in Romans," Hap said, smoothing the delicate leaf of paper with his gnarled hand.

Cara had known that he would have answers for her. She'd wanted to ask the questions the day before right after the service, but Holt had so unnerved her that she'd thought it best to keep her distance until he'd gone. Then this morning Hap had announced that Holt would arrive this afternoon as soon as Ace rose from his nap to "help with the heavy work," as Hap put it. Cara had decided to speak to Hap about Grover's sermon during the lunch break, and he'd already clarified much that had confused her. The old man pecked the paper with the tip of his forefinger.

"Yep, this is the passage Grover read yesterday. Now what is it that's got you stewing?"

Cara shifted close, and he moved over to make room for her at the end of the table. Bending low, she started reading to herself.

"There," she said, placing her fingertip on the page. "What does that mean, 'His elect'?"

Hap bent low, adjusting his glasses, but even as he looked,

he spoke. "Well, now, that just means believers. We'd say Christians these days, but the term wasn't in use back then."

Cara read the passage again, aloud this time, then went on to the end. "Huh. It doesn't say anything about sin."

Hap chuckled. "Well, now, it does and it doesn't. It talks about charges and justification, and those things have to do with sin, the committing of it and the forgiving of it. The point Grover was trying to make is completely valid, though. Here, let me show you."

His knobby hands flipped through the delicate leaves with swift surety. He took her through the book of Romans in a matter of minutes. Soon Cara's mind whirled with memorable phrases.

All have sinned and fallen short of the glory of God.

He is faithful to forgive.

He Who did not spare His own Son.

Confess with your mouth.

The last one bothered her greatly. "What does that mean?"

"In this case, it means declaring aloud that Jesus is your savior. In some other verses, it means to admit to your sins, your wrongdoings. That's the first step to salvation, admitting your sins and seeking forgiveness."

Saddened, Cara merely nodded and stared a little harder at the Bible. How could she confess her wrongdoings if it meant putting herself and her son in danger? She certainly wanted to. The longer she knew Hap Jefford and his grandsons, the more pronounced her guilt became, but then she'd think of the cold, doubtful look in Holt's eyes, and fear would overwhelm even her shame.

Restless and cranky, Ace kicked the wall next to the portable crib, letting them know that nap time had arrived.

"We better get out and let him sleep," Hap said, picking up the Bible. "We can continue this in the front room."

"Oh, no," Cara said, sidling in the other direction. "I have two more units to do." She jerked a thumb in Ace's direction. "I'll just get him down and head back to work."

Hap opened his mouth as if to protest, but the front door chime sounded, and he flattened his lips. "Best see who that is. Likely it's just one of the boys."

Cara didn't hang around to find out. Whether it was one of his domino buddies or a paying guest, she had work to do and thoughts to mull over, though what good might come of that, she couldn't imagine. This confession thing had her stumped. She couldn't even explain her predicament well enough to get answers without Hap or someone else tumbling to the very thing that frightened her most.

Feeling sick at heart, she went to the crib, bent and picked up her son. Cradling him against her chest, she carried him out to the laundry. After emptying both washers into the dryers, she took Ace back into the apartment, where she began to sway and croon. Drowsy as he was, Ace fought sleep for several long minutes before he relaxed into bonelessness. During that time, Cara kept thinking over and over how she could not be one of God's elect because she did not dare confess her sins. Much as she wanted the assurance that she did not live separated from God's love, she knew that if confession had to be part of it, she was doomed. For how could she tell anyone, let alone Hap or Holt, that she had run away from a mental institution?

Cara placed her palm against her son's forehead and felt the heat radiating off his skin. Irritable, Ace squawked and shoved her hand away.

"I can't go," she said, torn between disappointment and relief.

She'd managed to keep her lips sealed these past three afternoons while working with Holt, who'd been all things endearing, and she'd been looking forward to this midweek prayer meeting to which Hap had invited her. After all, God would still hear her prayers, wouldn't He, even if she couldn't confess her deception? He'd heard her before when she'd prayed for help. On the other hand, she wanted to confess so badly at times that she just didn't trust herself, not around Holt, at any rate, and especially not the friendly Holt who seemed so fond of her son now.

"What do you think it is?" Holt asked, smoothing Ace's hair with his big hand.

"Maybe we should be calling a doctor," Hap suggested.

"Office is closed," Holt pointed out. "We'd do better to take him to the emergency room in Duncan."

"He's cutting teeth," Cara said. "That and a case of the sniffles is all it is, but it's enough to make him too fussy for church. You two go on without us."

"Are you sure?" Holt asked, his brow creased with worry.

Cara almost laughed. Big, bad Holt Jefford. Let a kid steal his hat and he went all soft over him. She wished it didn't please her so much.

"He'll sleep and tomorrow he'll wake up fine."

"Well, if you're sure," Holt hedged.

"We'll pray for him," Hap declared.

"But meantime, if you need us, you call," Holt told her. "I'll set my phone on vibrate."

"We'll be fine," she insisted, settling into the rocking chair in the front room with Ace on her lap, "and we'll be right here holding down the fort when you two get home."

The men started for the door. Holt hesitated, looking back at her with a frown before following Hap out into the cold.

"They'll be fine," she heard Hap say. "'Sides, you got your phone. What'd we do before Ty got us them phones?"

She couldn't make out Holt's reply as they moved away. Then again, she couldn't make out much about him, period.

First he'd been downright standoffish, even grumpy, now he seemed to be making an effort to be friendly. He'd been a lot of help, too, cleaning drapes and carpets and so on, those chores that went beyond the daily tasks. Seemed like someone was always pitching in these days. Ryan had done the dinner dishes on Monday and Tuesday.

"Only fair," Ryan had told her when she'd protested, "since I'm eating your cooking."

Hap had said pretty much the same thing when he'd insisted on washing up this evening. He'd even gone so far as to claim that the hot, soapy water felt good on his arthritic hands.

Neither of them made her uneasy like Holt, did, though.

He still worried her with his pointed, perceptive questions and narrow-eyed stares, but it was more than that. She practically itched whenever the man came around, especially if he stood too close. She supposed it had to do with the times when she'd let down her guard with him and run off at the mouth, letting things fall that would be better left unsaid, like when she'd mentioned Aunt Jane and blurted the explanation of Ace as a nickname for her son.

At least she'd managed to cover, or so she hoped. E for Edward. Thank God she hadn't uttered the name Elmont. That information could lead to all sorts of trouble for her.

Ace stiffened up like a board in her lap, complaining about the mucus that clogged his throat and reduced his howls to croaks.

"Okay. Let's see if we can't get you a little relief."

Rising, she moved into the apartment, where she paused to shrug into an old corduroy coat that Hap had started insisting she wear. Even with the sleeves rolled halfway up, they covered all but her fingertips, but the big coat provided ample room for carrying Ace inside it against her chest. They hurried across the tarmac to their room to grab the little bag where she kept such things as baby vitamins and analgesic drops.

After she got the drops into him, cleaned his nasal passages and put the kettle on to steam atop the potbellied stove in the front room, Ace drifted off to sleep cradled against her in the rocking chair. His weight so numbed her arms that she carried him back into the apartment and laid him in the crib, thinking how much he'd grown in these past couple of weeks. He still slept peacefully an hour or so later when the men returned.

"How is he?" Hap asked at once, coming through the front door.

"Breathing easy and sleeping hard," she told him, tipping the chair forward as she got to her feet. "I'd better get him settled in for the night."

"I hate for you to wake him," Hap said. "Why don't you let him stay here in the apartment with me tonight."

"Oh, no, I couldn't," she insisted, shaking her head. "He'll expect me to be there when he wakes."

"But he and the crib are too much for you to manage," Hap began.

"I'll help her," Holt said, the front door closing behind him.

The protest rose automatically to her tongue. "No, no, that's not necessary."

He glowered at her. "I said, I'll help you."

She ducked her head in acquiescence, knowing that she'd have a difficult time getting the crib collapsed and across the tarmac with a heavily sleeping Ace in her arms. Irked, she followed Holt into the apartment where she slung on the corduroy coat. He moved to the crib, bent and easily lifted Ace into his arms. Hastily, Cara folded up the crib and together they moved through the kitchen and out the back.

Holt felt the warm little body snuggled against his chest and warmth seeped into his heart. The first time he'd held the boy, he'd marveled at his unexpected heaviness. Now, however, the little guy felt light as a feather. Holt supposed it was a matter of perspective. Ace no longer rated as a burden to be borne but, rather, someone to be shielded and protected. Holt wondered when that had happened.

Maybe it was seeing the usually good-natured imp fussing and unhappy earlier that evening. Or maybe it was simple proximity. Holt had come to appreciate the little scamp's usual sunny nature these past few days. It seemed to Holt that this boy needed the protection of an arm stronger than his mother's and so far as Holt could see, he happened to be the only one around capable of providing it.

That didn't mean Holt would be any less protective with his own family, however. He'd been protecting and caring for his family since the deaths of his parents, and he would not allow Cara Jane to hurt either of them. He wanted to believe that he had her all wrong, but Cara Jane *had* lied. Holt knew it, he just didn't know *how* yet.

He'd had real trouble staying in his chair while listening to Cara and Ryan chat in the kitchen earlier this week. The talk had been completely innocuous, all about how she'd prepared certain dishes and how she seemed to use fewer pots and pans than Charlotte did. The real problem had been how happy Cara Jane had sounded, how at ease the two of them had seemed with each other. Holt had wanted to march in there and demand that Ryan be as leery of her as he was himself, but he'd wanted to do that because he knew it would keep Ryan away from her.

The irony of the whole situation continually pricked Holt. He *knew* that she lied. That ought to have been enough to repel any feeling for her. Instead, he found himself drawn to her, even admiring the way she went about her work and how seriously she took her responsibilities as a mother.

How, Holt wondered, had he gotten into this mess?

More importantly, how did he get out of it?

He'd asked God that very thing tonight, but silently, which reminded him of the promise Hap had made earlier.

"We prayed for Ace tonight," Holt told her as he waited for her to get out her key and let them into her room. "Everyone did. We put his name on the general list."

"Thank you," she said, turning the key in the lock and pushing the door open. "I appreciate that. I really do."

Holt followed her into the closet and waited while she set up the crib with quick, familiar efficiency. It bothered him that the boy didn't have a proper bed and that she had to drag that contraption around with her all the time. Besides, where would Ace sleep if a paying guest needed the crib? One had been enough before they'd acquired a resident infant. He decided he'd best discuss the issue with Hap and see if they couldn't come up with a more permanent solution, then it struck him that he shouldn't be thinking of permanent solutions until he knew the truth about Cara Jane.

He lowered Ace into the freshly made bed, then stood by while Cara Jane changed his diaper. The boy stirred, complaining with whimpers and kittenish growls, then promptly dropped off to sleep again the moment she covered him with a blanket. Holt and Cara Jane crept back out into the larger room.

"He'll sleep until the medicine wears off," she predicted.

"You got enough to see him through the night?" Holt asked.

"More than enough. Besides, with all those prayers, he could be well before morning."

"Take that much stock in prayer, do you?" Holt asked idly.

She nodded and bent to swipe a wrinkle out of the coverlet near the foot of her bed. "I'd be foolish not to, considering."

The statement sounded unfinished to Holt, so he had to ask, "Considering what?"

She shrugged off Hap's coat and plopped down on the bed she had just straightened, kicking off her shoes and tucking her feet up under her. Holt watched her decide how much to say. Finally, she answered him.

"I was praying in my car when I came upon this place."

"You don't say?"

"Maybe that's not how it's properly done," she went on somewhat defensively, "but it was quiet, Ace was sleeping, and I was driving, trying to figure out what we were going to do." She broke off and glared at him. "Well, you talk to other people when you're driving, don't you? I've heard people say prayer is just talking to God."

Holt held up a hand, palm out, in concession. "That wasn't criticism. It was surprise."

She ducked her head, saying in a small voice, "You don't think I pray? Maybe you don't think I ought to."

"Of course I think you ought to pray," he told her. "I think everyone ought to pray. Fact is, I was praying for help the very minute you first walked in the front door."

She looked as astounded as he felt, her spine going ramrod straight, lips parting. Then she laughed, falling backward. "You don't say?"

Holt couldn't suppress a grin. "Hey, that's my line."

She studied him for a long moment, her pale head tilting to one side, before she abruptly sat up, declaring, "That's why you gave me the job, isn't it?"

He wondered how careful he ought to be in answering, then decided not very. She was too bright not to have tumbled to his misgivings already. "That was a big part of it," he told her. "In this family, we believe in the power of prayer, so when I asked for help and then I looked up to find you standing there hoping for work, well, how do I argue with that?"

Her gray eyes lost their focus for a moment as she thought that over, then sharpened again as she asked, "You said that was part of it. What's the other part?"

"Hap. He loves this place, believes he's called to it, but he can't keep it going alone, and I was at the end of my rope trying to help him."

She nodded, gaze averted. "I'm grateful no matter why you did it."

He thought she might say more, but when she didn't, he did, just to keep the conversation going. "So where'd you learn to pray?" he asked.

She shrugged and picked at a thread on the toe of her sock, which showed dazzlingly white against the dark bed cover. "My great-aunt was a praying woman."

"Not in church then," he said as much to himself as her.

She shot him a sharp glance, and then she lifted a shoulder. "My parents didn't like church. I guess they figured they'd have to clean up their act if they went to church."

"And your husband?" He didn't know why he'd asked; it just seemed important.

"Wouldn't even talk about it. His whole family thinks that church is just a scheme to get money out of them."

"Ah. I know those folks." Holt slipped his hands into his pockets. "They're the same ones who think the government ought to take care of the poor without bothering them about it."

"If I didn't know better, I'd say you'd met the…my in-laws."

"Can't say as I care to neither," he said, shaking his head.

"My sentiments exactly. The farther they are from me and Ace, the better I like it."

Holt's radar pinged. So she disliked her in-laws, did she? "I figured Charlotte would feel that way about Ty's family," he said conversationally, "but slay me if they don't fall all over themselves to please her. Could be because Ty's different since he met her, or different since he met the Lord."

"So he confessed, did he?" Cara Jane asked, face drawn into a woeful expression.

"Confessed?"

Her expression suddenly blanked. "His sins."

"Oh, I can testify to that," Holt told her happily. "I was there."

She seemed to wilt a bit, and it occurred to him that she must be tired. "I'll go and let you get some rest yourself."

"Thanks," she muttered, uncoiling her legs to get up and trail him to the door, "for everything."

"Carrying Ace over isn't anything," he said dismissively.

"It is," she insisted, "but I was thinking more about the help you've been giving me these past few days."

"That's no big deal, either," he told her magnanimously. "I just thought I should help out around here."

"I have to wonder why, though," she said just as he opened the door. The chill that flushed over him had less to do with the frosty temperatures than the cold edge of her voice. "It's not like I'm going to steal the curtains off the windows, you know."

He turned around in the open doorway, the hair on the back of his neck ruffling. "I never said you would." But he'd thought it a possibility, and she knew it.

Something flashed over her face, anger definitely, perhaps even hurt. "You," she said, "can be such a rat." Before he could even digest that, she put a hand in the middle of his chest and shoved. He reeled backward through the doorway, which she stepped into, blocking any re-entry. "You can tend to your own business from now on," she snapped. "I don't need your help anymore." With that, she shut the door.

He came within an inch of kicking it, but with Ace sleeping in the other room, he restrained himself. Confounded woman! She deserved his distrust, and he'd helped her in spite of it. He'd be boiled in oil before he helped her out again.

Halfway across the tarmac, he realized that was exactly

what she wanted, him out of her way. He stopped and looked back at her door.

That woman read him like a book. He knew that she lied; she knew that he knew it.

It was even more than that, though, and he'd be foolish not to admit it. Something sparked between them.

For some surely stupid reason, that made him grin. By rights he ought to be appalled and plotting how to keep his distance while still somehow ferreting out her secrets, but that wasn't going to happen. He'd be here tomorrow, whether she liked it or not, and maybe, just maybe, that electric spark which so unsettled the both of them would eventually set off an explosion big enough that he'd finally learn what secrets she held so close.

Beyond that, he dared not even speculate.

Chapter Eight

❧

"Is that an order?" Cara asked, keeping her tone light. She leaned slightly sideways, her hands linked together around Ace's waist to help balance his weight as he straddled her hip.

After almost a full week of working with Holt each afternoon, despite her every attempt to persuade him otherwise, she'd come to realize that his bark was definitely worse than his bite and that perhaps he did not actively dislike her, after all. That did not mean that he trusted her or that she could afford to trust him, and considering how much she was coming to actually like him, it seemed as necessary as ever for her to keep her distance. Yet here he stood on a chilly Saturday night, expecting to take her to dinner. She felt duty-bound to try to get out of it.

"No, it's not an order," he answered flippantly. "I don't give the orders around here, but that's not the point."

Cara rolled her eyes. "What is the point?"

"For one thing, you haven't been off this property since you got here."

"That's not true. I went to church last Sunday and to the park the Sunday before that, and last night I walked over to Booker's Store to buy diapers."

"You know that doesn't count," he retorted. "You need to get out, and you need to eat tonight, too, don't you? I certainly do." He pressed a hand to the center of his forest-green shirt, his eyes glowing deep olive in the muted light cast by the fixture outside her room.

"I can eat here. I've got food in the fridge." Bologna and yogurt.

"You're not really going to make me eat alone, are you?" he wheedled. "I don't like eating alone, and you won't like seeing the look of disappointment on Hap's face when he finds out you refused to take your turn for a Saturday night out."

She grimaced at that, instantly capitulating. "Not fair."

Holt laughed and stepped into the room as she turned and carried Ace deeper into the warmth. "Granddad has a way of worming into your affections, doesn't he?"

Cara nodded, resigned. "I mean, really, who could not like Hap Jefford?"

Holt gently pushed the door closed. "You'll get no argument from me on that score. Grandma always said the goodness of the Lord shines through him."

Cara thought about that, aware of a wistful envy, which she pushed away at once. Wishing did no good. She'd learned that years, decades, ago.

"Now," Holt said, clapping his hands together, "what do you need? Coats? Diaper bag? A little arm-twisting?"

She laughed because he was being so charming and his usual high-handed self at the same time, a very dangerous combination. Oh, why hadn't she pled a headache or some other illness? But she knew the answer to that. Her lies were already eating her alive; she just couldn't bear another.

"Come on," he coaxed, "the Watermelon Patch is waiting."

The Watermelon Patch, she'd learned, was the local catfish restaurant. Justus called it a "dive," but even he vowed that better food could not be found around these parts. She acknowledged, if only to herself, a certain desire to see the place. Besides, she never won when it came to Holt. It irritated her, but the man always seemed to get his way. Maybe because she really didn't have the heart to fight him. Shying away from the thought, she waved a hand toward the dresser and the small satchel atop it.

"Um, I'd better stick an extra diaper into the bag." She looked down at her jeans and rumpled T-shirt. "And change my clothes."

"Naw, you're fine," Holt insisted, grabbing up the diaper bag.

She brought her free hand to her hip and gave him a blatant once-over. "I don't see you going out in your work clothes."

He set down the diaper bag and lifted both hands in surrender. "Okay. All right. Fine. Change, by all means. I'll watch Ace."

Miffed despite getting her way for once, she snatched her car keys from the bedside table and tossed them at him. He trapped them with both hands in midair.

"Move the car seat instead."

He tipped his hat, lips quirking. "Yes, ma'am."

"It goes in the backseat," she lectured, "and make sure it's anchored properly."

"I'm on it." This time he pushed his hat down more firmly on his head. "Any other orders before I go?"

She just rolled her eyes at him. He went out the door grinning. She couldn't keep a smile from breaking out on her own face—until she remembered that she had nothing suitable to wear.

Holt had the child safety seat securely anchored in the center of the back bench of his double-cab pickup inside of five minutes and spent the next ten pacing back and forth beside the truck while his stomach rumbled.

Spinning Cara Jane's keys around on his index finger, he had to wonder why she never drove her car. Not only had she walked to church last Sunday—in sandals, no less—she'd admitted just minutes ago to having walked all the way over to Booker's Grocery west of downtown to buy diapers.

It had been spitting rain last night in near freezing temperatures, and thinking of her and Ace out on foot in that weather made the hair stand up on the back of Holt's neck. No matter what route she might have taken, at least half a block of it lacked a sidewalk, which meant she'd have had to walk on the narrow shoulder of the street, carrying Ace. All it would have taken was one careless driver, or even a good driver with a slick tire, and they could have had a catastrophe too horrible to contemplate.

The door opened and Cara Jane walked through it, Ace on her hip and the diaper bag hanging from her shoulder by the strap. Holt nearly swallowed his tongue.

She wore slim, pink pants, cropped at mid-calf, with a purple tank top, those flirty purple sandals and her denim jacket. With her hair tied back with a purple scarf and narrow gold hoops dangling from her earlobes, she looked like she'd just walked off a movie screen. It struck him suddenly how tan she was. Even now, in the dead of winter, her skin glowed pale gold.

At some point in her not-too-distant past, Holt mused, Cara Jane must have spent time in a tanning bed. He supposed that in the rainy northwest a tanning bed might not be such a bad idea to keep the doldrums at bay. Still, something about that scenario struck him as patently un-Cara Jane.

The notion flitted right out of his head as she strode toward him. She looked so good that just keeping a stupid grin off his face required all of his concentration. As she neared the truck with Ace, Holt dashed over and opened the back door for her. Then, realizing that she'd have to climb up inside to lift Ace into his seat, Holt promptly took over that chore, only to learn that buckling a kid into a safety seat required a degree in puzzle solving, especially when said child objected.

Cara Jane marched around the rear end of the truck, dropped the bag onto the floorboard and climbed up into the backseat on the other side to show him how it was done. While holding Ace in the seat with her forearm, she got the harness over his plump little shoulders, fit two pieces of metal together with one hand, positioned the latch with the other and somehow connected all three.

As soon as he heard that telltale click, Ace stopped struggling and settled down.

"Now you're cooperative," Holt teased, nipping the end of the boy's nose with the knuckles of two fingers. Ace favored him with a broad grin. "Whoa! Is that a tooth breaking his gums?"

"It is," Cara Jane confirmed in an I-told-you-so voice. She started backing out of the truck cab. Seeing how difficult that could be in those tall shoes, Holt jumped down and jogged around to help her, but she hit the ground just as he got there. She stumbled, her shoulder bumping him in the chest.

"Oops." He automatically closed his arms around her, steadying them both.

Instant awareness shot through him and apparently her, too, because they practically repelled each other, bouncing apart as if they'd both been hit with cattle prods. They each sought refuge in pretense, her smoothing her hair, him repositioning his hat.

Their aplomb somewhat restored, they both turned toward the truck, only to reach for the door handle in the same instant. The thing might have been electrified so quickly did they yank their hands back.

Finally, reaching wide around her, Holt gingerly opened the door and stepped back, hovering uncertainly until she'd climbed up into the front seat. He made his way around to the driver's side, where he paused long enough to close his eyes and blow out a steeling breath before getting this undoubtedly ill-advised venture under way.

Cara looked around at the ramshackle building, marveling that it hadn't fallen down around their heads already. A "dive," indeed. This place—which actually did sit in the midst of a currently barren watermelon patch about a half mile outside town—had been cobbled together with incongruent bits and pieces, some metal, some wood, some cement, some plastic. Nothing matched, not even the shingles on the roof.

The rough floors waved unevenly across heights varying by inches. Tables and chairs had been crammed into every available square inch of space, each and every one of them occupied.

The waitress, a hard-looking bottle blonde named Joanie, stuck their small party at a wobbly table that sat dead center of the passage between the two dining rooms, one of which contained an old-fashioned glass counter where the proprietor collected payment. Traffic had to squeeze by them, but at least the spot came with a high chair.

Ace loved the busy, humming place. He banged on the table with both hands, thrilled that he could make it tip, unless Holt, who sat across from him and on Cara's right, leaned on it with his elbows. He indulged Ace by keeping his hands in his lap. Cara's concern hinged more on her son's safety than his pleasure, however.

"I only see the one exit," she pointed out, leaning close to Holt in an effort not to be overheard, if one could be overheard in all this din. People talked and laughed, clinking their dinnerware and shouting across the crowded room at one another.

"That's because there is only one exit," he said in a false whisper.

"But what if there's a fire?" she muttered, an event that looked not only possible but entirely likely to Cara, given the smoke that belched from the stack pipe outside and the number of people crammed into the building.

Holt spread his hands, grinning at her. "Then there would be lots of exits. Cara Jane, Ace could punch his way through that wall right there." She had to admit Holt had a point. "Besides," he went on, "half the windows in the building would fall right out if you so much as tapped on them."

Someone behind her chuckled and exclaimed, "It's not a matter of *if* a fire breaks out, little lady, it's a matter of *when*. That's why they serve the drinks in these big old jugs."

"That's right," Joanie concurred, plunking down quart jars of iced tea. "In case of a fire, you just put it out your own selves with these."

The room bubbled with laughter. The locals obviously didn't worry overmuch about building or fire codes. Cara consoled herself with the idea that this place had been around for over thirty years, or so Hap's friends had said.

Joanie dried her hands on the seat of her skintight jeans. "How many?"

Cara looked up at the waitress in confusion. The woman had drawn her shortish hair into a ponytail so tight that it slanted her eyes. "How many what?"

"Pieces of fish."

"I'll have four," Holt announced.

"Not you," Joanie said, swatting a hand sideways. "I know how many you want. You always have the maximum."

"And then he eats everything else that's leftover in the building," someone who obviously knew Holt well put in.

Holt sighed loudly while everyone else laughed at his

expense, but Cara could tell that he didn't really mind. He sat among friends here.

Joanie looked at Cara expectantly.

"How big are the pieces?" Cara asked.

"You're teeny. I'll just bring you two," Joanie decided, looking her over.

"Three," Holt countermanded. "I'll eat the extra."

Joanie cut her heavily lined eyes at him. "You sure you don't want to just go the limit on both plates?"

He spread his hands in easy capitulation. "Might as well."

"Four and four it is."

"Well, my cobbler's safe tonight," some fellow teased.

"I don't know," Holt said, deadpan. "I'm powerful hungry."

They laughed and made jokes all over the room about eating faster and guarding their food. Joanie, meanwhile, pointed to Ace.

"What about him, sugar? You want to order something for him? We got some applesauce, and Cookie will mash up some potatoes and beans for you, if you want."

"Applesauce," Cara decided, smiling wanly. "I brought along some jars of baby food anyway."

"I'll be right back with your corn cake." Joanie slid away, swimming a curvy path in and out among the tables.

"Corn cake?" Cara asked Holt.

"Best corn bread this side of Georgia," he bragged.

"Oh. I like corn bread," Cara said, brightening with the memory of Aunt Jane's sweet batter, baked or sometimes fried.

A chair scraped and a female voice asked, "You ever gonna introduce us to your girl, Holt?"

He jerked, then sent a look straight into Cara's eyes. That look said, "Sorry. I'll try to set the record straight." Cara surreptitiously sucked in a deep breath. He cleared his throat and half turned in his chair, hanging one elbow over the back of it.

"'Fraid I can't call her mine, Angevine. This here is Cara Jane Wynne. She works for Hap down at the motel, and since she's taken Charlotte's place, we figured she deserves Charlotte's night out."

A heavyset redhead in her mid- to late thirties materialized at Cara's elbow, offering a surprisingly dainty hand. "Nice to meet you, Cara Jane. I'm Angevine Martin. I saw you in church on Sunday, but you were gone when we got out the door."

"Oh, uh, Ace got restless, so we left a little early."

"Ace, that's her boy there," Holt said with a wave of his hand. Winking at Ace, he added, "He likes singing and hats."

Angevine giggled, glancing at Holt's bare head. He'd left his hat in the truck, predicting correctly that there wouldn't be room for it inside, but the curving sweep of his hair showed where it could usually be found.

"Well, that's something y'all have in common," Angevine gushed. Then she shocked Cara by patting her on both cheeks. "I'm just so happy to meet you!" She patted Holt on the shoulder as she pranced back to her seat. "First Charlotte, now you. I guess Ryan'll be next. About time the Jefford kids started settling down."

As murmurs of agreement spread throughout the room, Holt sent Cara another apologetic look, but he said nothing more to refute the idea that the two of them made a couple. Cara understood from his expression that anything he might say would simply add fuel to the fire at this point. She tried not to cringe, but she'd gladly have crawled under the table just then. Fortunately, talk turned to descriptions of Charlotte's wedding, with comments flying about everything from the food to the decorations to the groom's family.

"Never seen the like," an elderly fellow said on his way to pay his check. "They came in here with caterers and florists and decorators." He flew a hand into the air, adding pointedly,

"In limousines. Every one of 'em in limousines. They'll pro'bly build that new house with lumber shipped in by limousine."

He ambled off without waiting for any rebuttal, which wouldn't have come at any rate. Holt just chuckled and shook his head, while conversation abruptly shifted to the house that Charlotte and her new husband planned. One woman had heard that they'd bought sixty acres from a ranch west of town and were building a twenty-thousand-square-foot mansion.

"It's eight thousand square feet and thirty acres," Holt corrected. "They bought the Moffat place out east of the school grounds. Already pulled down the old house."

"That didn't take much, I warrant," someone put in, amidst gasps about the true size of the house.

"Nope. Just hooked a chain to the door lintel and the bumper of my truck," Holt confided. "Ty was going to send a wrecking crew, but I told him, 'Why bother?'"

Joanie brought the corn bread, still steaming from the oven. Holt set aside a piece to cool for Ace while someone asked whatever happened to Old Man Moffat. Several people debated the exact year of his death until Holt gave it to them around mouthfuls of buttered corn bread. Cara hadn't yet managed to split her piece, so hot it blistered her fingertips and so soft it fairly crumbled when touched.

"I remember because the drought was so bad that year they couldn't get the grave dug," Holt said to the room at large. "They called Daddy out to break up the ground with one of his big bits. It was the year before he died."

The atmosphere immediately took on a solemn feel.

"Good man, your daddy," a voice grated.

The sentiment echoed softly around the room.

"Good man."

"Good 'un."

Holt wiped crumbs from his shirtfront into his lap, but Cara knew memories of his father played fresh in his mind. On impulse, she slipped a hand beneath the table, intending to give him a slight touch on the knee. Instead, he dropped his hand just then, so she gave it a sort of fumbling squeeze. She meant it to be a simple gesture of sympathy and understanding, but Holt's long fingers closed over hers and suddenly they were holding hands, palm to palm. He never so much as lifted his gaze to hers, but their clasped hands hung there between them for several heartbeats while talk began to swirl around them once more and Cara's breath heated inside her lungs.

Joanie appeared, sliding plates and bowls and baskets onto the table, giving Cara the perfect excuse to break free. She quickly snatched up a corner of cooled corn bread and poked it into her mouth, humming with self-conscious appreciation. Just then, Joanie placed a bowl of applesauce in front of Ace, and everyone at the table reached for it.

Holt got to the applesauce first, sliding it out of Ace's grasp just before disaster could strike, leaving Ace with a smidge of applesauce on the tip of one finger, which Ace promptly popped into his mouth. Laughing, Holt scooted closer to the table, shunted aside his own food and spent a good five minutes spooning applesauce between Ace's smacking lips while Cara mashed big, meaty slices of fried potatoes with spoonfuls of pureed beef and peas.

Watching Holt feed her son touched Cara. No other man had ever done such a thing for him. Not his father, who'd seemed rather impatient and frightened of his tiny newborn son in the short time they'd had together. Not his uncle, who barely acknowledged his nephew's existence, and not his grandfather, who was much too important to be bothered with such things.

As soon as the last of the applesauce disappeared, Holt set to his own dinner while Cara split her time between feeding Ace and herself. It amazed Cara how much that man could eat, and it made her wonder if she shouldn't start cooking larger quantities. Her own meal tasted very good, but it was filling fare, which meant that Holt had plenty with which to gorge himself. No one seemed to think a thing of him eating off her plate.

"Waste not, want not," he quipped with a wink, helping himself to pieces of whole fish, potatoes and red beans, for which she'd never developed a taste despite her aunt's attempts to feed them to her. He did leave her half-eaten coleslaw untouched, though he scoffed down every bit of his own before lolling back in his chair, replete. By the time Holt had eaten his fill, Ace's head bobbed, his eyelids drooping to half-mast.

"Now I see why you don't like to eat alone," she teased. "One meal isn't enough for you."

"Nailed that, did you?" He patted his lean middle, adding, "I've about reached my limit tonight, though." He sat up straight again, glancing at Ace, just as Joanie delivered steaming bowls of peach cobbler. "I may even have to share my dessert with Ace."

"Oh, no, you don't," Cara said, pushing away her own dish. She just didn't have room. "No sweets for him. If you fill him with sugar he won't sleep tonight."

"He's asleep sitting up now," Holt pointed out, scraping back his chair.

"Guess you'll be wanting these to go," Joanie said, dropping the check and scooping up the cobblers again.

Holt nodded and picked up the bill. "I'll just settle this while you get Ace ready. Then we'll take our dessert and head out."

Cara rose to begin stuffing Ace into his outdoor layers. While she did so, folks kept coming by to offer personal welcomes.

"So good to meet you," said a complete stranger whose name had never even been mentioned to Cara.

"Hope you'll be happy here in Eden," a sweet-faced, elderly matron crooned. "Right fine little town."

"You couldn't do no better than to land with the Jeffords," pronounced a lipless fellow in a gimme cap and ragged coveralls. "Good people."

"You couldn't do no better than Holt, either," the plain-looking woman on his arm said. Cara opened her mouth to dispute the connection, then closed it again as the couple moved off.

"If you'll be wanting to get into the Ladies' Auxiliary, hon. I'll put your name up," Angevine Martin told her with a giggle just before she swamped Cara in a pillowy hug.

Cara hardly knew what to say to these well-meaning folk, so she just smiled and nodded and smiled some more. Joanie dropped off the cobbler in one large disposable cup. Holt returned at about the same time and hoisted Ace into his arms.

"Y'all come back now," a voice called, and Holt swept the owner a wave.

The trio started toward the door. Just then a young man half rose from his chair, cupped his hands around his mouth and bellowed, "Hey, Holt! Could you go back to wherever you got her and get me one?"

Cara's face instantly flamed. She felt sure it must clash with her outfit. Then Holt's strong arm ushered her through the door. At the same time he yelled back over his shoulder, "Sorry. One of a kind!"

They carried laughter with them into the cold air and, in Cara's case, a secret sense of delight.

She told herself that it would be foolish to hope for something personal with Holt Jefford. First, he didn't trust her in the slightest. Second, his lack of trust would be fully validated if he ever learned the truth. He would most likely hate her then or, at the very least, turn away.

She didn't even want to think about the third reason, but she forced herself to face it.

The day that the Elmonts discovered her whereabouts, she'd have to run again. How could she leave her heart behind her when she went?

No, it would be far better never to even start down that road. She could only hope that it wasn't already too late.

Chapter Nine

Holt kept his arm looped around Cara Jane as he escorted her toward the truck, Ace snug in the curve of the opposite elbow. He told himself that it was because of the cold, but in truth he just liked having her close to him. That should have terrified him, but something else seemed to override his good sense.

For one thing, the assumptions of the townsfolk concerning a romantic development between him and Cara Jane didn't trouble him nearly as much as they should. The fact that he hadn't realized that everyone would figure Cara Jane for his girlfriend troubled him more than the assumption itself. He hated that she had been embarrassed by it. If he'd been thinking at all, he could have prepared her for what she would encounter, but he'd been too intent on getting information out of her to consider beyond that.

"I should've warned you about all the carrying on," he told her. "There's always lots of teasing and talk going back and forth. Everyone pretty much knows everyone else, so any newcomer is of interest."

"I understand," Cara replied, glancing around at the crowded parking lot, if an expanse of bare, dusty ground punctuated with trees, piles of debris and a propane tank the size of a small whale could be termed a parking lot. "Looks like the whole town's here tonight."

"Naw, just half of it," Holt quipped, relieved that she didn't sound offended by all the talk. "The other half came last night. This place is sort of the town's unofficial social club."

"I see. Tonight's crowd is certainly a friendly bunch."

"They are that," he agreed, but his conscience wouldn't let him ignore the real issue, so he added, "I just never realized how much interest there is in the romantic status of the Jefford siblings."

Cara shrugged, saying nonchalantly, "Obviously your sister's wedding is still in the forefront of everyone's mind."

"Obviously." He felt sure it was more than that, however, and he wanted her to be prepared, so as they reached the truck and he slipped his keys from his coat pocket, he said, "You can bet, though, that the main topic of conversation for the immediate future is going to be the two of us and this little guy right here, including his father and why he's out of the picture."

Holt looked down at her, saw the sad resignation behind those soft gray eyes and felt like a complete heel. He'd hoped to shake loose some new information by spending time with her, not to make her an object of speculation or, worse, gossip. Had he thought for two minutes about something other than his suspicions, he'd have known this would happen.

"I'm sorry," he said. "I should have realized what you were in for."

He kept expecting her to be upset with him, but she stood there between him and his truck, shivering inside her meager denim jacket, and broadcast forgiveness with a wan smile. A spark burst to flame inside his heart and spread warmth throughout his chest.

"Ace's father is dead," she said matter-of-factly. "It was a freak accident. He stopped to help another car broken down on a busy highway overpass. The witnesses all thought it was a woman driving, a young one, probably, which is the only thing that makes sense because I can't imagine Addison stopping otherwise. Then, somehow, he fell, and that's all there is to say."

Holt knew the truth when he heard it. He knew pain, too, even pain as layered as hers.

Nodding, he opened the truck and deposited a flagging Ace into his seat. Poor little guy didn't even bother protesting this time, just turned his head into the corner and closed his eyes. To Holt's surprise, Cara left him to perform the buckling process, hurrying around to climb up inside the front cab. Aware of how the cold must be affecting her, he joined her as quickly as he could, not at all offended that she turned to check his handiwork while he started the engine and got them moving.

They drove in silence for a moment before something she'd said triggered a thought. "Seems like that woman he'd stopped to help should've hung around after he fell, doesn't it?"

Cara shrugged. "I'm not sure she even realized it had happened. No one actually saw what went down."

"Huh. That doesn't sound a little suspicious to you?" he asked.

Cara turned her head toward him, meeting his glance. "I don't see why. The police did try to track her down, but the car turned out to be a rental."

"Didn't they follow up on that?"

"I can't imagine why they would, really. Addison didn't have any enemies."

"That you know of," Holt replied. Suspicion—or was it something else, something outside himself?—tightened his chest. He had to ask, "Have you considered other reasons for her behavior?"

Cara bowed her head, her face shadowed by the dim light

from the dashboard. "You mean, that maybe he was cheating on me, that she was his girlfriend and had called him for help that day, then sped away after the accident because she didn't want it to come out?"

"Something like that," Holt admitted, his stomach starting to churn.

Cara looked out into the dark landscape passing by her window and softly admitted, "It was a distinct possibility." She looked at him. "But what difference does it make now?"

Uncomfortably wounded on her behalf, Holt fiddled with the temperature gauge on the heater, which had only just begun to blow tepid air. "I admire your attitude," he said, "but if you'll forgive my saying so, your late husband doesn't sound like much of a prize."

She leaned her head against the window, admitting raggedly, "Our marriage wasn't the greatest. But it wasn't the worst, either. It wasn't much of anything at all. But he gave me Ace. That's reason enough to grieve him."

"Yes, it is," Holt agreed gently.

The heater blew warmer now, so he turned it up, knowing that she couldn't be comfortable in those summer-weight clothes, clothes she could not have had much use for back in Oregon. If that's where she'd truly come from.

Truth and lies in one pretty little bundle, he thought.

He wished for everyone's sake that he could believe otherwise, that he could just accept what she'd told them and trust that nothing from her past would reach out to bite him and his family. Unfortunately, he just didn't know how to turn off the uneasy feeling that she hid something important.

All in all, he *had* learned new information about her tonight, he mused. He'd learned that she'd been hurt by her late husband and unhappy in her marriage but that she had managed to let go of her pain and be thankful for her blessings.

He could have done without that knowledge. It made him feel ashamed of his suspicions while doing nothing to lessen his concerns.

The rest of the trip passed in warm silence, both lost in their own thoughts.

After they arrived back at the motel, Holt carried in Ace for her. It had almost become a ritual with them, one he liked more than seemed wise, but he simply could not stand by while she struggled with the boy's dead weight and maybe even woke him in the process.

Cara Jane thanked Holt for his help.

"No problem."

It was their standard interaction lately, but as he was going out the door again, she suddenly said, "I had a lot of fun tonight."

That surprised him. He'd sensed her embarrassment and discomfort at times during dinner, and his guilt about that returned forcefully; he knew he'd be talking to God about it later.

For now, with his hand on the doorknob and the door ajar, he choked out, "Me, too."

"I know I'm the newcomer," she went on, "and a subject for gossip, but I somehow felt a part of the community tonight. Does that make sense?"

It made a lot of sense. Eden was a friendly town, and the Saturday-night crowd at the Watermelon Patch treated the place like one big community dining room. That Cara had felt a welcome part of that lightened Holt's conscience a bit and, at the same time, tightened his chest.

He turned to face her, a lump rising in his throat at the soft look on her face. He couldn't have gotten a word out to save his life, so he did the only thing he could think of. He leaned in and pressed a kiss to her forehead.

Before he could do worse, he quickly backed through the door, taking with him a trepidatious heart and the vision of her sweet, wistful smile.

Cara and Ace attended church with the Jeffords the next day. This time they rode in Holt's truck and sat up front in the usual Jefford pew. She'd argued that it might be wiser, considering the assumptions about the two of them, for her to make the trek on foot, despite the biting cold, and sit apart from the Jeffords, but Holt had decreed the plan pointless. Hap had dismissed the whole thing.

"People will talk," he'd said. "Let 'em. God knows the truth. Better than we do, even."

That did nothing to ease Cara's conscience. The more she got to know the Jeffords, the worse she felt about lying to them, especially to Holt. Her feelings for him had taken an alarming turn the night before, reinforcing her determination to keep as much distance between them as possible.

Holt had left his hat in the vehicle when they went in to church, a wise decision because, even though Cara had managed to maneuver Hap into a seat between her and Holt, Ace continually lunged back and forth between them. He treated Hap as a human bridge, often pausing during transition to dispense hugs and pats.

To Cara's relief, none of the Jefford men became impatient or seemed the least disturbed by the constantly moving little body. Ryan, sitting on the end next to Holt, even seemed to feel a little left out and at times tried to entice Ace onto his lap, but though Ace smiled at Ryan and flirted with him, he did it sitting with his back flat against Holt's chest. At least, Cara consoled herself, Ace was happy and quiet, and that allowed her to pay some attention to Grover's message.

It turned out that he was preaching a series from the book

of Romans. She didn't understand much of what he read aloud, but she did get the premise that the created have no right to complain to the Creator about how they are made. Another idea, however, not only confused but troubled her, that those pursuing righteousness via the law "stumbled" by not pursuing righteousness through faith.

What did that mean, she wondered, to pursue righteousness through faith? And what was this law about which the writer spoke?

She needed to speak to someone about this, someone who might not become too suspicious if she hedged or changed the subject. As before, Hap would be her first choice, but after the last time they'd spoken of such things, she feared giving away too much with him.

During the final part of the service, when the congregation stood and softly sang while Grover gently exhorted those with needs to come forward for counseling and prayer, Cara felt an almost overwhelming compulsion to rush down the aisle and throw herself onto her knees, but she stayed put out of fear. Later, when she stood shaking hands with Grover, the notion of speaking to him in private hit her. When she quietly asked if that might be possible, he promptly suggested a time the next afternoon, then added that he'd take care of it with Hap. Feeling somewhat lighter, Cara went out to meet the others.

Holt had carried Ace from the building, seeming as comfortable as if the boy were his own. Cara's heart lurched when Ace lifted his hand to press it against Holt's mouth, as he often did with her. Holt first kissed Ace's palm then blew a raspberry against it, eliciting joyous giggles. Cara knew in her heart of hearts that Addison would not have been so easy with their son, that his affection would not have been doled out so unstintingly and without motive.

The sadness that had descended on her after that first, terrified grief suddenly threatened to envelope her once more. Then Holt caught her eye, smiled and waggled Ace's hand in a wave.

Thank You, God, she instantly thought. *Thank You for my son. Thank You for bringing us to this place and these people.*

She wanted to ask that He allow them to stay, but after the lies she'd told these good men, she dared not ask for what she knew she did not deserve. For the first time, she began to wonder what she and Ace would do when they left here. They couldn't live forever in a tiny kitchenette. Ace could not grow up sleeping in a walk-through closet. Even if the Elmonts didn't find them, she and Ace would have to move on at some point. A growing boy needed a real home, and it fell to her to provide that. Somehow. Somewhere. She wondered how she could possibly do that on the run. If only the Elmonts had not filed for custody of her son....

Her shivers had less to do with the cold than the sudden bleakness that filled her.

Cara bowed her head, sitting forward on the edge of Marie Waller's flowered sofa in the living room of the modest parsonage next to the church. Ace played on the rug between her feet. After coffee, a plate of sliced fruit and cheese and a solid forty minutes of conversation, during which the pastor's wife had quietly disappeared, some of Cara's questions had been answered. She now understood that the Law referred to the Ten Commandments, and that only through grace could anyone hope to live up to its standard.

Unfortunately, receiving grace required confession of one's sins, and she'd come no closer to being able to do that. All during the previous night, she'd wrestled with the possibility of confessing all, but that would only put the Jeffords in an untenable position. She couldn't expect them to keep her secret, so she could only confess if she could move on, but to where? To what? God knew she wouldn't get far on the money she'd managed to save thus far.

Grover had urged her to unburden herself to God, but she'd already done so, more than once, and somehow it only seemed to heighten her need to tell Hap and Holt and Ryan the truth. She felt trapped in a vicious circle of fear, guilt and lies.

Now, as the round, jolly pastor prayed aloud, tears leaked from Cara's eyes, welling up from her heavy heart.

"Father, You know Cara's burdens, and we're both trusting You to help her carry them. Help her see that her need for You is greater than whatever is holding her back from full surrender. Wrap Your arms of love and protection around her. Resolve these issues that are weighing so heavily upon her, and bring her fully into Your will for her life. Meanwhile, O God, make all of us who love You a blessing to her and Ace. In the name of Your Holy Son, Jesus the Christ, amen."

Sniffing and wiping her face, she gulped back her tears and took a deep breath before lifting her head. "Thank you, Pastor."

"I wish you could find the peace you're seeking," he told her gently.

She shook her head. "Maybe I just don't deserve it."

"None of us do," he insisted, "but thankfully that didn't keep God from making a way for us to have it. You should know, in case you decide to talk particulars, that I'm bound to confidentiality by the sanctity of my office. Nothing you tell me will leave the room."

She fully realized that he meant what he said, but she thought of Hap and Grover's deep friendship with him and knew that she couldn't ask the pastor to keep her secrets. "I'll think about it," she hedged.

She bent and swung Ace up onto her lap to get him into his outer clothes. Once that had been accomplished, she drew on

Hap's old coat over her denim jacket and rose. "Thank you for your time."

"I'll be praying for you," Grover said, taking her hand as he led her toward the door. "Whatever the trouble is, my dear, know that you have real friends here who will stand by you."

He could say that, of course, because he didn't know what it was that she dared not confess. Nevertheless, she treasured the fact that he'd said it.

"I appreciate that. Thank you again."

She hurried out onto the porch at the front of the house, smiled a farewell and shifted Ace onto her hip so she could descend the steps. The sky looked fittingly flat and gray, and a slicing wind swirled, clacking the bare tree branches and slashing any exposed skin to ribbons. She wished she'd worn Hap's old gloves or at least a scarf on her head. At least Ace was warm inside his layers and fleece hoodie.

Hugging him close, she crossed the street and turned toward the motel. She hadn't gone ten yards when she heard a vehicle approaching from behind her and then a beep. Turning, she found Holt lowering the driver's side window on his truck.

"What are you doing?"

"Heading back to the motel."

He put the truck in Park, got out and opened the back door before stepping up on the sidewalk and reaching for Ace. "Get in."

Cold, she yielded her son and trotted around to the passenger side. They'd agreed after church yesterday to take care of switching the car seat later, so the thing still sat anchored in the center of the back bench of his truck. Thankful for that, Cara basked in the warm air blowing from the heater while Holt buckled Ace into the safety harness.

Holt slid in across from her a few moments later, snapped his own safety belt and pulled the gear lever into the proper position to move forward, but then he paused with his foot on the brake, hung a wrist over the top of the steering wheel and turned to face her. "I can't believe you went out in this cold on foot."

"I had things to do," she told him defensively, stung.

"You should have waited for me to drive you wherever it is you needed to go."

"I didn't want to take up your time with it," she retorted.

"Then you should've taken your own car," he snapped.

Cara folded her arms mulishly. "I couldn't. The car is making an awful racket and I'm afraid to drive it, even a couple of blocks."

He just looked at her for several heavy heartbeats before facing forward again and depressing the gas pedal. "What was so important you had to go out anyway?"

She took her time answering that, mostly because she didn't want to lie to him. In the end she just told him without regard to consequences, muttering, "I wanted to speak to the pastor— I mean, Grover."

Holt shot her a glance, then carefully blanked his expression. "Okay. But why take Ace out in the cold when Hap's more than willing to watch him?"

Her defensiveness fading, she bit her lip, then had to admit, "I honestly didn't even think of leaving Ace with Hap."

"Well, it's time you started thinking about it." His expression softened, taking the sting out of his words. "You're not alone in the world, Cara Jane, whatever you may think."

The gallantry of that, coupled with her conversation with the preacher, threatened to move Cara to tears once more. She cleared her throat and said, "I'll keep that in mind."

Holt gave her a quick nod, then, "I'll take a look at your car first chance I get."

She bit her lip. "That's not necessary. After my next paycheck I'll—"

"*I'll* take a look at it," he interrupted, driving straight across the back lawn of the motel. "Then we'll see." He scraped a look over her, adding, "Ask me, you ought to be investing in a real coat and some winter clothes before you do anything else."

She hadn't asked him, and she knew she wouldn't be spending her hard-earned money on clothing for herself. She had no one but herself to blame for her inadequate wardrobe. Even though she'd had to sneak clothing out of the Elmont house over a period of days during her Christmas holiday furlough from the clinic, things that wouldn't be missed, she could have included some warmer articles. She just hadn't been thinking at the time, and now she paid the price by suffering the cold in order to accumulate funds in case she had to flee. The car being a necessity, she made no further protest about him taking a look at it; instead, she silently endured the jostling of the truck until it came to a stop next to the patio.

Thanking Holt for the ride, she slid out onto the ground. They both climbed up into the back from opposite sides to free Ace from his harness. Once unbuckled, however, he reached for Holt rather than his mother.

Cara told herself that Holt was nothing more than a fresh face for her son, but deep inside she feared Ace had become as fond of Holt Jefford as she had.

This was another complication that she had not foreseen. Indeed, the list of her failures seemed to grow hourly.

First, she hadn't appreciated the fact that Eddie would undoubtedly look for her around Duncan. Second, she hadn't planned for an emergency, like the car breaking down. Third, she'd underestimated the work involved in the job she'd taken on. If Hap and Holt and even Ryan were not good enough to pitch in, she'd be in way over her head by now. In fact, if her employers had been anyone else, she'd probably be on the street by now! In addition, she hadn't truly understood how arduous it would be to keep Ace with her all day long. Just the logistics of that were exhausting. Besides all that, she'd lied about her identity, where she'd grown up, where she'd come from, and why she'd struck out on this fool's mission to begin with, even about what she'd run away from. Worse, she hadn't counted on becoming so fond of the Jeffords that her conscience would get busy and eat her up like this.

It seemed to Cara in that moment that the best thing she could do was just hit the road again.

In a car that she didn't trust to drive another mile and with limited funds. Right.

No, she'd dug this hole by herself. She'd have to find a way to climb out on her own, too.

In the meantime, all she could do was pray that Eddie and the Elmonts didn't show up with a shovel.

Chapter Ten

Holt tossed the broken hunk of metal into the bed of the truck. He'd spent most of the morning figuring out the problem with the engine and getting to it. Now he had to find a replacement for the failed part.

After stripping off his filthy gloves, he tucked those into a green plastic bucket affixed to the inside of the truck bed by an elastic band. Next, he unsnapped and peeled off his quilted coveralls to cram them into the bucket on top of the gloves, leaving him standing in jeans and a white, long-sleeved insulated knit shirt. His hard hat went into the bucket last, becoming a protective lid of sorts.

Reaching into the rear compartment of the truck cab, he took out his heavy canvas coat and quickly donned it before sliding beneath the steering wheel. A billed cap, bearing the silhouette of an old wood derrick spouting the words "Jefford Drilling and Exploration," rested on the dash. He pulled that on, settling the bill just so, before turning the keys that dangled from the ignition switch.

The truck engine rumbled to life. As he wheeled the vehicle

around the lot to the side of the drilling platform, he lowered the window and hung an elbow out of it.

"You men pick up around here, thread, dope and cap enough pipe to get us through the next couple days, then clock out and go on home. I'll see you in the morning. And don't forget to padlock the gate."

The crew waved a few grimy salutes and nodded their yellow hard hats. On one hand, it was busy work to keep them from losing a full day's pay. On another, with enough pipe threaded and ready for coupling and all hands on the deck when they started to drill in the morning, they ought to be able to make up for lost time, provided he got the engine up and running again.

Lots of drilling sites operated twenty-four hours a day, seven days a week, but those belonged to larger outfits that primarily serviced the major oil companies. Holt preferred to work for himself. He paid good money for geologists reports, made his own assays and negotiated his own leases on percentage, then sold any resulting oil to middlemen who, in turn, passed it to refiners. That meant sinking his own funds into the drilling operations, most of which came up dry. He had enough wells operating to keep the business going, though, with three portable rigs and two crews, one of which was punching holes up in the panhandle right now.

Holt prided himself on being able to offer steady work, with very little actual downtime. He took just enough of the profits to keep himself housed, fed and clothed, turned a good bit back into the business, banked as much as possible, and felt pretty good about providing incomes for a number of families. Working for himself meant doing a lot more than scouting leases and supervising operations, though. It also meant looking for replacement parts and working on his own equipment when the need arose.

He'd drive to Duncan in search of the part first, he decided, but if he couldn't find the thing there he'd have to head to Lawton or points even farther afield, which could make for a very long day, indeed. He used his cell phone to call the motel and let Hap know where he'd be. Hap had a dozen questions, so Holt spent almost the entire drive explaining the situation, including the fact that he'd leased his extra rig.

Though a cantankerous old thing, the third rig in his operation provided backup when another went down due to catastrophic mechanical failure of some sort. On the other hand, it mostly sat around in a field out behind his barn rusting and attracting field mice. He'd figured he might as well make some money off it, even if said money only went to repairing one of the two newer rigs.

With small operations like his, things went wrong about as many days as they didn't, but wrong could usually get made right in a relatively short period of time. Those days when nothing went right, Holt accounted as "patience" days, days the Lord set aside to teach him patience. Nobody had to tell him that he was a slower learner.

Today, he almost felt grateful for the distraction. He hadn't been able to get Cara Jane off his mind even for a minute these past couple days. He couldn't help wondering what she'd needed to talk over with Grover. She seemed open and curious about spiritual matters, but he doubted that she had a full understanding of them. Could a Christian woman lie to his face? To Hap's? At this point, just one thing kept him from demanding some straight answers, the fear that he might actually have her entirely right—or entirely wrong. He couldn't decide which would be worse.

He sensed her disquiet. Something bubbled and roiled beneath that sweet, feminine surface of hers. Like a frightened bird poised for flight, she seemed to long for the warmth of the nest and yet fear it at the same time. On Tuesday, he'd asked her point-blank if she had something troubling her. She'd straightened, smoothed her brow with her wrist, her hands clad in rubber gloves, and looked him in the eye. He'd held his breath, but then her gaze had fallen away. She'd shaken her head and gone back to work. He'd wanted to fold her up in his arms, but whether to shake her or calm her to his touch as if she were an abused puppy he didn't know.

For the umpteenth time, he put her out of his thoughts. That lasted, mostly, right up until he found the needed part at, praise God, the very first place he tried.

Deciding that God must have deemed this a "take it a little slower" day, Holt tooled up Highway 81 to the drive-in burger joint and ordered a double cheeseburger, onion rings, extra-large cola and hot apple pie. The food hadn't even arrived when an electrifying impulse hit him.

Why not, since he had a little free time, drive by Cara Jane's old address? He could find it easily enough, and maybe just seeing where she'd grown up would offer some insight. Of course she'd supposedly left there long ago, but what did he have to lose? Someone might be able to give him some clue to the mystery that was Cara Jane Wynne. Besides, with his busy schedule, he might not have an opportunity like this again for a long while.

Half an hour later, he pulled over to the curb in front of a modest older home to polish off the burger and rings. The pie, he reasoned, would eat as good cold as hot. He cleaned his face with a napkin and got out of the truck to walk up the broken path to the low porch.

On the southeast side of town, the small house had been cheaply built back sometime around the Second World War. It had been minimally maintained. The hipped roof showed the most age, sagging in the center, but the original porch had been replaced at some point with a concrete pad that lent a contrasting air of permanence to the plain, square posts which held up the overhanging roof and clapboard siding painted a dull, uninspiring gray. The original front door had long since been traded for a dark, paneled, Spanish-style one that flatly did not belong. Lack of attention had let the yard go to dirt, except for the evergreen shrubs that flanked the walkway and an enormous cedar towering over all.

Holt knocked and shortly found himself greeted by a friendly young couple.

"I wonder if you might remember a girl who used to live here, a Cara Jane Wynne?"

As expected, they shook their heads and told him they'd recently rented the place from a Mr. Rangle.

"He might know her," the young man suggested.

"Or Mrs. Poersel might," the woman said, pointing next door to a better maintained white house with updated siding and gleaming metal roof. "Poor old thing's bedridden, but she loves to visit. Sent her nurse over here to invite me in before we even had the car unloaded. I'd guess she's been in that house fifty years or more."

Holt thanked them and walked next door. A jolly black woman in pink nursing scrubs and braids answered his knock, introduced herself as Gladys and let him ask his question before guiding him through a rabbit warren of musty knickknacks and worn furniture to a centralized bedroom and a thin, old woman who looked like she'd disintegrate if an errant puff of air should hit her. The house felt like an oven.

Mrs. Poersel half reclined in the center of a high, four-poster bed, wearing a frilly pink bed jacket and headband to contain wiry but thinning white hair cropped at chin length. A bed tray straddled her meager lap, and atop it rested a plate containing a sandwich. She was attempting to eat it with a fork and knife, her gnarled and spotted hands trembling with the effort.

Gladys walked around to the far side of the bed. "This young man wants to ask you about someone," she said, unceremoniously picking up the sandwich and sticking it beneath the old woman's nose.

Mrs. Poersel snapped off a bite, whereupon Gladys dropped the sandwich and left the room. Mrs. Poersel smiled at Holt while chewing punctiliously behind clamped lips.

He removed his cap and held it before him, saying, "Cara Jane Wynne? I understand she used to live next door."

Mrs. Poersel swallowed and broke into a smile so wide it nearly dislodged her dentures. "My, yes!" She rested her knife and fork on the edge of the lap tray. "I do miss her. What fun we had." She beamed up at him. "Would you like a sandwich? I love a good sandwich, though they're hard to eat properly, aren't they?"

Holt had always figured that the proper way to eat something was the most obvious and efficient. "No, thank you, ma'am. I've had my lunch already. Very kind of you to offer."

Giggling, she asked, "Did you know about the berries?"

"The berries?" Holt shuffled his feet, momentarily lost; that or the heat was frying his brain. "Oh! You mean collecting blackberries on the side of the road?"

Mrs. Poersel laughed. "She could make the best pies in the world! Didn't you love her berry pies?"

Lost again, he could only glance around in the vain hope of enlightenment. "Cara Jane? At what? Twelve or thirteen? I— I thought she left here before high school."

Mrs. Poersel clapped her hands to her sunken, wrinkled cheeks. "I must mean later on!" Her dark eyes twinkled, the pupils so big that they barely left room for the irises. "No, wait. You're talking about the girl. Pale, pale hair? Sad smile?" That sounded like Cara Jane, so he nodded. Mrs. Poersel laughed, reminiscing. "She used to catch lightning bugs and keep them in a jar. She'd run all around the yard, almost like one of them, flitting here and there. She was the daughter her aunt never had, you know."

"Her aunt?"

"Mmm. My very best friend in the whole world. Lived for that child. Well, someone had to care for her, didn't they? Whatever happened to her? Wound up like her mama, I fear."

"No, ma'am," Holt hastened to reassure the elderly woman. "Cara Jane's just fine. She works for my grandfather and has a little boy of her own."

The old woman threw her head back in horror. "Cara Jane! Now, she never mentioned that boy to me." Shaking her head, she clucked her tongue. "I suppose I might have judged her." She suddenly looked to Holt, a beatific expression on her face. "Society's strictures have their place, and the Good Book is solid, but one does learn as one grows older to take a broader, kinder view."

Holt had the feeling that they were striving to communicate from alternate universes, but he bobbed his head and said, "Yes, ma'am."

"Now, Cara Jane, whatever her faults might have been, she was one for doing one's best, for making do and being thankful. But it's not enough for some. I gather her sister was like that."

"You mean her brother," Holt corrected, relieved to find that the Cara Jane whom he had come to know hadn't changed all that much from the Cara Jane remembered by her old neighbor.

"Yes, I suppose I do." The elderly woman's gaze wandered around the room as if seeing it for the first time. "There was a brother, wasn't there? Though mostly it was just the girl. Sweet little thing with that blond hair always hanging in her eyes. I wonder what became of her." Before he could remind her that Cara Jane worked for his grandfather, Mrs. Poersel gusted a great sigh and exclaimed, "I do so miss Cara Jane!"

"Maybe I could bring her to visit soon," Holt suggested. He wondered just how long the old dear would remain in this world; she looked that pale.

She hunched her thin shoulders. "Wouldn't that be a treat!" Her gaze wandered off again. "My own children were older, you understand, but Mr. Poersel was still alive then. Did you know him? Worked fifty years in insurance."

Holt shook his head. "I'm sorry, no."

"Those were good times, if only we'd known it, but difficult for a single woman. What else could she do?" Mrs. Poersel shook her head and seemed to answer her own question. "Cleaning other people's houses was the only work she could get after the war, you know."

Holt felt sure they weren't speaking of Cara Jane now, but he just smiled. Gladys came back into the room then, walked over to the bed, picked up the sandwich and offered it to the old woman, who retrieved her knife and fork before taking another bite.

"Now you keep eating," Gladys instructed kindly, "while I show this young man out." She smiled at Holt, saying, "The least little thing tires her."

A glance showed the old girl all but asleep in her plate already. Holt thanked her for her time, but she didn't respond. Gladys smiled and turned him toward the door. "She gets awful muddled. Did you find out what you needed to know?"

"Yes, I think I did."

"That's good," Gladys was saying. "Then, you both got something out of it. I know she enjoyed the visit, even though it's not one of her better days. You come back some other time, she might be a little clearer."

"I just might do that."

"Don't you be too long about it," Gladys warned, adding with a smile, "You stay warm out there now."

He didn't think he'd ever be cold again. Sweat trickled down between his shoulder blades as he made his way out into the refreshing January air. Filling his lungs with the sweet, clean briskness, he set out jauntily for the truck. He doubted Mrs. Poersel would even remember him when she woke next, but he felt he ought to return with Cara Jane, out of gratitude if nothing else.

Mrs. Poersel hadn't made a whole lot of sense in there, but she'd confirmed to his satisfaction that Cara Jane had, indeed, lived in that house next door. And chased lightning bugs with a jar. He could just see her, skinny little arms and legs pumping, blond hair flying out behind her. As he slid into the truck, he remembered what Cara had said about her drug-addicted mother and Mrs. Poersel's comment about Cara Jane following in that parent's footsteps. Suddenly overwhelmed by gratitude, he bowed his head.

"Thank You, Lord. Because she didn't turn out like her mama. She's more like those lightning bugs than poor old Mrs. Poersel can imagine. Thank You for that."

After lifting up Mrs. Poersel and thanking God for finding the part he needed to fix the drilling engine, he ended his prayer. Then he peeled the paper wrapping off the fried pie and had himself a little celebration as he headed back to Eden.

Cara Jane decided to attend prayer meeting that evening, even though it clearly meant leaving Ace in the church nursery. Holt couldn't help feeling that they'd made progress. Not only had he confirmed that she had, indeed, lived in Duncan, she seemed to be loosening her grip on the boy just a bit. Holt supposed it was understandable, having lost her husband in a puzzling accident, that she would cling to Ace and want to keep him with her, but it was not always the wisest course for Ace himself—or for Holt. Once she felt comfortable leaving Ace in Hap's care, Holt could spend more time focusing on his own business.

She balked a bit when they handed off Ace at the nursery door.

"He's fine," Holt assured her, taking her hand and tugging her toward the fellowship hall and the sanctuary beyond it, attached via a narrow hallway.

Her steps lagged for a bit, then she fell in next to him, her hand never leaving his.

Holt smiled, thinking of that little girl who had chased lightning bugs with a jar and of the half promise he'd made to Mrs. Poersel. Given that, the statement that followed seemed entirely sensible.

"I drove by your old house today."

Cara Jane stumbled and nearly fell. He grabbed her with both hands, noting the sudden paleness of her face.

"Y-you did what?"

He tried not to frown, but alarm bells clanged inside his head. "I had to make a trip to Duncan and I drove by your old house."

She leaned back against the beige wall, and he could see her pulse racing in the throb of veins at the base of her throat. "Why did you d-do that?"

He shrugged, his hands still hovering about her upper arms. "Just wanted to see where you lived."

She gulped but managed a wobbly smile. "Never was much to look at."

He drew his hands away, tucking his fingertips into the hip pockets of his jeans. "I spoke with a Mrs. Poersel."

Cara Jane gasped. "Mrs. Poersel is still alive?"

"Barely. How old is she, anyway?"

Cara Jane thought about it, her eyes flitting side to side as she appeared to calculate the years. "I'd guess mid-nineties anyway."

"She said she knew your aunt," Holt prodded.

"Yes." Cara Jane dropped her gaze. "The house actually belonged to her. My aunt, I mean."

"I take it they were good friends."

"Very good friends," Cara Jane confirmed with a nod, "although Mrs. Poersel was quite a bit older. How ironic that she should outlive my aunt by so many years."

"When did your aunt die?" he asked, trying to keep his tone conversational.

"Oh, before my fourteenth birthday," Cara Jane said.

"Is that why you moved away?" He sounded like an inquisitor, even to his own ears.

Again her gaze dropped. "Yes."

The piano began playing in the sanctuary. Cara Jane looked in that direction.

"Shouldn't we go in?"

"In a minute," he said, aware of a rising anger. Why did she do this to him? What was she hiding? Could he not have one full day of peace about this situation? "Mrs. Poersel would like to see you."

"Oh?"

That single syllable, false and wary and weak, told him how little the idea pleased Cara Jane. It didn't exactly thrill him, either. He'd thought that he'd settled something today, fixed at least one small piece in the puzzle, but the emerging picture suddenly made no sense to him.

"I have the feeling that sooner would be better than later," he told her firmly, "if you know what I mean."

Cara Jane swallowed. They both knew that she couldn't refuse. "I see."

Feeling a little ill now, he pressed on. "How about Sunday, between Ace's nap and the big game?" Hap had planned a Super Bowl party, partly because Charlotte and Ty wouldn't be joining them after all. Ty's mother had been rushed into gall bladder surgery, so naturally Ty and Charlotte had felt that they should stay close to her for the time being.

Cara Jane said nothing for a long moment, but the sound of singing reached them, and she looked once more toward the sanctuary door. He felt the longing in her, the yearning. "Fine," she said, sounding exhausted. Pushing away from the wall, she started for the sanctuary.

Holt watched her for an instant, torn between grim relief and keen dread. Then he followed her.

"Sunday it is, then."

"Sunday," she whispered.

He had the distinct impression that he'd just sentenced her to a cruel and unusual punishment. Perhaps both of them.

Chapter Eleven

Cara saw that she had entered the sanctuary at the front behind the piano. Avoiding eye contact, she kept one shoulder against the wall as she walked to the nearest empty pew and sat down on the end. Holt moved past and took the seat immediately behind her. Thankful for that much distance, she somehow managed to hold on to the edge of her composure, despite the trembling in her limbs.

She didn't sing, but she smiled at the woman in front of her who passed her an open hymnal. After the song, Grover rose to speak for a moment before dismissing them to small group. Cara, fighting off panic, barely registered a word, but she soon found herself being swept back the way she'd come, right into the large room they called the Fellowship Hall.

Earlier she had noticed that a shuttered window opened into a large kitchen along one side of the bland room. Of more immediate interest now, however, were the folding chairs arranged in circles of nine or ten seats. As people began filling them, Holt stepped up and lightly grasped her elbow.

"There's a mixed group forming over here."

She let him steer her to a chair and soon found herself sitting next to him and across from a couple about his age. The woman leaned forward and said a soft "hello." Angevine Martin came by, giggling and squeezing Cara's shoulder. Cara tried, hoped she'd managed, to smile. To her surprise, Holt took charge of the group.

"Any requests?"

A middle-aged man, sitting with arms and legs crossed, immediately began to speak about his impending divorce. He went on for several minutes, and Cara noted the soothing, supportive comments of the others, but she felt paralyzed, apart from the group.

Perhaps it was best that way, she thought tiredly. On Sunday next, her aunt's best friend would undoubtedly expose her lies and end her time in Eden.

Even in the midst of her terror, Cara tried to apply analytical logic to the situation, but the pall of doom hung so heavy over her that she could barely form coherent thoughts. Her wisest course might be simply to run, now, tonight, but the idea brought such enormous pain that the inherent fallacy of it seemed incidental. She had too little money accumulated, an undependable vehicle and not even a glimmer of a plan this time, but that all paled in comparison to her grief and disappointment. Her only option seemed to be to make that visit to Mrs. Poersel and endure whatever came of it, however terrifying.

God help me, she prayed in mechanical silence. *Oh, God, please help me.*

Several others around the circle voiced prayer concerns. Holt suggested that they pray silently then let him close them. Several people immediately slipped off their chairs and onto their knees, bowing their heads over the seats they had vacated. Cara followed suit and immediately felt overcome by a presence other than her own.

She began to cry out silent apologies to God, her tears flowing into the space created by her folded arms.

I'm so sorry! I didn't realize how hard it would be to lie, but what can I do now? Holt will report me, and even if he doesn't, I don't want to involve anyone else in my problems. I only want to make a good home for my son. Help me! Oh, please help me! I shouldn't have done it. I just didn't know what else to do. I'm so sorry. Please don't let Holt and the others hate me. At least if it all comes out, then You can forgive me, and I want that, but please, please don't take my son. Please don't let them lock me away and take my son. Oh, God, I'm so sorry!

She all but forgot about the others around her, until Holt jolted her into awareness by speaking aloud. With simple, homespun eloquence, he praised God for His mercy and kindness, addressed each request, mentioned several concerns of the wider church and even touched on some national issues.

Then he broke Cara's quivering heart, saying, "Lord, there's a lady in Duncan, Mrs. Poersel, who's about reached the end of her road. I ask You to ease her way, and I thank You for this touchstone to Cara Jane's past and pray that her visit will bring Mrs. Poersel the same measure of joy that she and Ace have brought to my grandfather and me." He went on to seek blessing for everyone in the room and their families. He asked God to use the church for His purposes and, as other voices in the background fell away, closed in the name of Jesus.

Cara hastily dried the last of her tears but kept her gaze averted as Holt's hand curled beneath her elbow, lifting her to her feet. He held her back with just a squeeze of his fingers as others began to move away. Some spoke to him, and he replied in jocular kind, until the two of them stood somewhat apart from the dwindling group.

Tilting her face up with a finger pressed beneath her chin, he looked down worriedly into her eyes. "Are you all right?"

She rubbed her nose, trying to hold back a sniff, and put on the best smile she could muster. "O-of course."

He frowned down at her, obviously not buying it. "I don't know what's eating you up inside, Cara Jane, but you've got to realize by now that my family and I will do everything in our power to—"

"You can't help me!" she declared, pulling away. Realizing what she'd said, she tried to cover. "B-because I don't need help. Besides, the Jeffords have already been generous enough."

Mouth flattened, jaw working, he shook his head. She could see his frustration, knew he bit back words he'd prefer to spew.

"I'm sorry, Holt," she whispered, daring no further explanation.

After a moment, he slipped an arm around her, turning toward the nursery wing. "Let's get Ace and go home."

Home, she thought bleakly. But only until Sunday.

She knew that she wouldn't run. She didn't have the heart. At least not before she'd seen Mrs. Poersel. After that, she didn't know what would happen, but she felt she owed that visit to her aunt's old neighbor. And Holt.

Over the next three days, Cara kept as much distance between herself and Holt as possible. By mutual agreement, they decided not to "repeat the mistake," in Holt's words, of their previous Saturday night out together. Both stayed in, Holt whiling away the evening with Hap and Ryan, Cara watching television with Ace in their room.

Work helped distract her mind from the agreed-upon visit with Mrs. Poersel, but it did not stop Sunday from coming. Cara skipped church, saying truthfully that she hadn't slept well the night before. What was the point in going when doom hung like a pall over everything and confession remained impossible?

All too soon, she found herself riding in Holt's big truck, Ace happily babbling to himself in the rear seat, as the miles fell away and her secret dread built. With no comfort to be found from any other source, Cara prayed in silence almost incessantly during that long drive, but as the truck turned off of 81 onto Bois D'Arc Avenue on the south side of Duncan, she lost the concentration required even for that. Morbid curiosity and desperate longing mingled with her dread as they made the familiar right onto 10th Street.

They crossed Highway 7 and drove past West Stephens Avenue. Much remained the same, but a new brick house had replaced the old Downing home. She marked another notable change as they passed West Duncan. The hues were different. Once all the houses had been painted basic white. Now there were subtle shades of tan, gray and gold in the mix and even a smattering of more vibrant hues.

Holt parked the truck in front of Aunt Jane's house. Cara stared for long seconds at the dark, ugly door and cold concrete slab that had replaced the front porch. She much preferred the old wood porch and the door with the big window in it. The drab gray paint of the siding seemed to reflect her mood and confirm that this was not the same place she had known.

Saddened not to feel the tug of home, Cara opened the truck door and slid out. Oddly, despite the obvious changes, Mrs. Poersel's house seemed as familiar and solid as Cara's memories. Preoccupied, she didn't even realize that Holt had taken Ace from his car seat until they joined her.

"Her mind doesn't seem to wander so much as skip all over the place," Holt warned. "Don't be concerned if she doesn't recognize you right off."

Cara's lips curved wryly. The possibility of Mrs. Poersel failing to immediately recognize her counted as the least of her worries.

Holt's big hand came to rest in the small of her back, propelling her forward without actually applying pressure. Within moments, admitted by a competent and friendly private nurse, Cara found herself standing in Mrs. Poersel's hot, crowded living room.

It felt like a sauna, albeit a cluttered one. Yet, even the clutter retained something of Mrs. Poersel's natural elegance. Cara had always known that the kind neighbor's bric-a-brac items were the cheapest to be found, but that had not prevented them from assuming a certain dignified, even magisterial, ambience once placed by Mrs. Poersel's graceful hand.

Gladys, the nurse, arrayed in flowery purple cotton and athletic shoes, put her hands to her ample hips and smiled at them, her teeth white in her dark face, her many short, beaded braids clacking cheerfully.

"Well, now this is fine. Ya'll come on back. It'll make her day." She patted Ace's back, addressing Holt before moving away. "It's sweet of you to bring your family by, hon."

"Oh, we're not—" Cara began, only to break off as Gladys disappeared into the dining room, or what used to be the dining room. It had become, Cara quickly saw, a sick room, complete with four-poster bed, dresser and, lamentably, IV pole. Holt frowned at that IV pole, even as Mrs. Poersel—a smaller, frailer, more wisened version than the one Cara remembered—beamed at them from the bed.

"Sugar, that nice young man's come back with his wife and baby," Gladys announced, going to plump the pillows at her charge's thin back.

"Oh, actually, he's not my husband," Cara said quickly. Gladys turned a surprised look on her, prodding Cara to add, "He's my boss."

Holt turned his frown on Cara, stating flatly, "I'm not her boss. Cara Jane works for my grandfather."

Gladys chuckled. "Okay. Whatever you say."

At the same time, Mrs. Poersel reached out a cadaverous hand, asking, "Did you say Cara Jane?"

Cara put aside her embarrassment and stepped forward, announcing forthrightly, "It's Cara Sharp, Mrs. Poersel. Remember me? From next door?"

"Cara? Little Cara?"

Her face wreathed in a smile, Mrs. Poersel reached out for a hug with both arms, one of which trailed an IV line. Cara stepped forward, gingerly enfolding the fragile old lady. She felt less substantial than Ace, like autumn leaves swirling in the breeze. Cara straightened, tears clouding her vision, and heard Holt quietly ask the nurse, "How is she?"

"Not long for this world," Gladys announced baldly. "She'll soon be going home to Jesus. Won't you, old darlin'?"

Mrs. Poersel lay beaming against her pillows. "Not soon enough," she rasped. Then she moved her hands together weakly. "Cara. Oh, my child, you're here in her place. I can't thank you enough."

Cara bowed her head, cringing inside, wishing she hadn't come, so glad now that she had. She reached out to lightly clasp a finely knobbed and veined hand. "Can I do anything for you?"

Before Mrs. Poersel could answer that, Holt asked, "Are you in pain, ma'am?"

Mrs. Poersel looked at Gladys and actually laughed.

"Ain't modern medicine grand?" Gladys quipped. It had obviously become something of a joke between them.

"Not with this contraption," Mrs. Poersel said in cheerful answer to Holt's question, waving the IV line. "Mostly what I am is old. And glad to see Cara. So glad." Her gaze shifted to Ace. "Is it your baby?"

Cara glanced at Ace. Big-eyed, he stuck two fingers into his mouth and warily looked around him. Holt had, thankfully, stripped him of his hoodie.

"Let me introduce you." Cara reached out, and Holt delivered the boy into her arms. She shifted him near the bed. "This is my son, Ace."

Mrs. Poersel studied him longingly. "Isn't he beautiful? Reminds me so of Albert."

"How is Albert?" Cara asked just to be polite. She only vaguely remembered Mrs. Poersel's rotund son.

"Waiting for me in heaven with his daddy," came the winsome reply. "Heart attack. Never did take care of himself. Cara Jane always said I spoiled him." Mrs. Poersel giggled and shrugged her delicate shoulders as if it were a great joke.

Cara was almost afraid to ask about the daughter, but she couldn't not do so now. She remembered Linda the best, though both Poersel siblings were decades older than her. "And Linda?"

"Very well. Retired." One gnarled, ivory hand wavered slightly. "Traveling the world."

"She just went to the church to drop off a cake for the fellowship supper," Gladys corrected with a smile, "but she's done some traveling all right. You name it, she's been there."

"Married well," Mrs. Poersel went on complacently, looking to Holt. "I hope she comes before I die." She fixed her gaze on Cara then, asking plaintively, "Will you pray that she comes home before I die?"

"I will," Cara said softly, glancing at the nurse, who merely shook her head. When Cara looked back to the bed, the sight of Mrs. Poersel with her hands folded and her snowy head bowed shocked Cara. Did the old dear expect her to pray at that very moment? Cara looked helplessly to Holt. He stepped up beside her an instant before his large, heavy hand covered her nape.

"Gracious heavenly Father," he said, his deep voice gentle and strong, "I thank You for Your loving kindness. Thank You for the place You've prepared for Your servant, Mrs. Poersel. I know You will welcome her with open arms in the company of her loved ones, but not until her daughter returns to this bedside. Thank You for Your generosity and patience in this, Lord, and for giving us this visit with an old and beloved neighbor. In the name of Your holy Son, amen."

"Eddie!" Mrs. Poersel exclaimed the moment Cara raised her head. "His name's Eddie, isn't it?"

Cara sneaked a glimpse at Holt, who seemed to accept this bizarre pronouncement with stoic calm. "Oh. Uh. My brother, you mean?"

"Cara Jane would be so proud of you both," Mrs. Poersel said. She smiled at Ace then, seeming to sink in on herself. "He's so beautiful. Makes me think of Albert."

Gladys sent them a meaningful look. Gulping, Cara nodded. "It was very nice to see you again, Mrs. Poersel."

"I miss her so," Mrs. Poersel sighed, her eyes closing. "All of them. I miss them all."

Holt slipped an arm around Cara, turning her toward the doorway with Ace. They navigated the crowded living room with Gladys trailing.

"Thank you all for coming," she said, standing patiently while Cara wrestled Ace into his hoodie. "You've made her last hours a little brighter."

Suspecting that Gladys had been nothing short of a Godsend to her old friend, Cara impulsively hugged the other woman, who surprisingly teared up.

"She done nothing but talk about your auntie since he's here last," Gladys said, waving a hand at Holt. "It's just the Lord's pure blessing that y'all came when you did. Now don't worry about her none. She's going straight to the mansions."

They parted with smiles and banked tears.

It hadn't been nearly as bad as Cara had feared. Sad, yes, and yet oddly uplifting, too. Glad she had come, unbearably relieved, she stepped out into the chill day.

"In my Father's house are many mansions," Holt said softly.

Cara faced him, the January temperature quickly cooling her overheated skin. "What was that?"

"It's from John 14," he told her, looking down into her eyes, "the very words of Jesus to His followers, the King James version. 'In my Father's house are many mansions: If it were not so, I would have told you. I go to prepare a place for you.'" He looked back to the house. "I'm glad to know her mansion is ready."

Cara marveled at this description of heaven. She could almost see Mrs. Poersel gliding through halls of marble and gold as if made for them, her earthly keepsakes replaced with valuables beyond description. Was Aunt Jane now living in one of those mansions that Jesus had prepared? A simple woman with simple tastes and simple wants, did she now enjoy unimagined luxury?

Yes, Cara believed she did.

And Addison? Her mother?

Cara closed her eyes, unable even to think the answers or to form the question that laid most heavily on her heart, the question concerning herself.

"When she speaks of Cara Jane, she means your aunt, doesn't she?" Holt asked, jerking Cara back to the moment.

Limp with relief, her emotions raw and her heart heavy, Cara could not lie to him again. "Yes," she answered simply.

"And Sharp is your maiden name."

"Yes. My maiden name."

Nodding, he ushered her down the steps and along the sidewalk, Ace snuggled against his chest.

"Thank you for bringing me here," Cara said once they reached the truck. She looked back at the house standing next to the Poersels', admitting, "I thought it would feel like home, but it doesn't."

"Is that why you were afraid to come?" he asked. Then, before she could even begin to formulate an answer, he mused, "Our fears never have as much power as we think they do." He tilted his head, as if listening to the sound of his own words again.

In that moment, she could almost, *almost,* believe them.

Holt was as disappointed as everyone else that Charlotte and Ty had not, after all, made the much-anticipated trip from Dallas for the big football championship game. Tyler had apologized profusely.

The family made do with an impromptu get-together of Hap's friends at the Heavenly Arms. Marie Wallace, Grover's wife, supplied her famous chicken lasagna, and Teddy Booker came with a Crock-Pot full of hot apple cider. It helped that Cara and Ace joined the party, with Ace happily beginning to lurch from lap to lap as soon as they arrived.

"Just like a real kid," Justus declared.

Cara blushed at this impolitic statement, compelling Holt to squeeze her shoulder. She'd been through a lot, seeing her old neighbor at death's door that afternoon. Receiving a smile for his efforts, he trailed her to the sofa and sat down next to her, remembering only as he settled himself how Charlotte and Ty had done the same thing and how everyone had known that they were drawn to each other even then.

He didn't want to be drawn to Cara. It hardly mattered now, for drawn he was. Once again buoyed by a visit with Mrs. Poersel, Holt lodged another tiny piece to the puzzle, a maiden name, and then put the whole mystery away to enjoy himself. Why not?

No one really cared a fig about the Super Bowl game except Ryan, but it gave them all something to do, something to celebrate, a reason to come together. Holt felt strangely content, oddly hopeful, and finally he faced the truth he'd been avoiding.

He wanted to let go of his suspicions and just trust Cara.

Cara Jane Sharp Wynne. He smiled, thinking of that little girl and the lightning bugs.

She seemed to enjoy the game, though she obviously knew next to nothing about football. Ryan proved only too happy to enlighten her, and she allowed him to do so with quiet indulgence. When Ace dropped off to sleep against Holt's shoulder, she rose, intending to take the boy out to their room and call it a night.

"You stay and enjoy your game," she urged, but with the boy already asleep in his arms, Holt wouldn't hear of it.

After carrying Ace out to the room, Holt worked quietly and efficiently with Cara to get the boy into bed. Then she turned, before he did, to move back into the outer room. Suddenly they stood face-to-face in the near dark, and somehow his arms were around her, those dainty hands of hers resting just above his elbows. He felt his heart stop beating and his head lowering toward her upturned face. At the last moment, Ace flopped over in bed, bumping against the wall, destroying the moment and restoring sanity. Holt cleared his throat as Cara glided away.

He took his leave quickly after that, and during the long night that followed, he pondered what he'd learned. It should not have been so important to him that her veracity had been proven, at least in this one area, by their visit with Mrs. Poersel. His relief felt entirely too profound, almost guiltily so, which meant that somehow he'd allowed himself to become attached to her.

Suddenly Holt could no longer be certain whose secrets were more dangerous, Cara's or his own.

Chapter Twelve

Holt finally found the time to take a look at Cara's car on Tuesday. Due to predicted precipitation, he parked the little foreign job beneath the drive-through at the motel for protection while he worked on it. He need not have bothered as the day turned bright and clear, if chilly. A quick adjustment stopped the clattering of a lifter arm, but he found another, more troubling issue that, had it manifested itself while Cara had been driving, could have resulted in disaster.

Though a pretty good mechanic in his own right, Holt knew he'd need help replacing a damaged pulley used by the serpentine belt that drove the engine. He called his old pal Froggy Priddy, of Froggy's Gas and Tire, the only mechanic's garage in town. Thankfully Froggy had little trouble getting his hands on the replacement part. An even greater blessing came when they discovered that they wouldn't have to completely remove the belt in order to replace the pulley. In less than two hours, they had adjusted the tension on the belt.

With the engine idling, Froggie crawled beneath the front end to check that all had been aligned properly, while Holt bent over the open engine compartment, tightening bolts and silently thanking God that Cara—he had stopped thinking of her as Cara Jane after their visit with Mrs. Poersel—had not found herself stranded or, worse, in an accident. As if summoned by the mere mention of her name to the Almighty, Cara appeared at Holt's elbow.

"It sounds wonderful!" she exclaimed, clapping her hands together. "The racket's gone!"

Holt straightened, smiled and nodded, tickled to see her so pleased, but when he opened his mouth to explain the greater ramifications of what he'd discovered, she struck him dumb by hopping up on tiptoe and throwing her arms around him in an exuberant hug.

"Mmm. Thank you so much!" She dropped back down onto her heels, grinning up at him. "You don't know how relieved I am. How much did it cost? I've put a little money back."

"Uh…" He couldn't remember what he'd been about to say to save his life. "It…needed an adjustment basically."

"That's all? Can I pay you for your labor, at least?"

"No. Uh-uh. No way."

Laughing, she clasped her hands together in the center of her chest before throwing him a kiss with a sweep of her arm. With that she danced away, beaming with gratitude.

He hadn't had a chance to tell her about the other issue, but somehow he didn't mind. So the repair would wind up costing him a couple hundred bucks. That made it a huge bargain, which he'd been quite willing to take on even before she'd stunned him with that affectionate display of gratitude. She'd seemed almost giddily happy since their visit to Mrs. Poersel, and he had no intention of dimming that smile, even if it did sometimes reduce his brain to a quivering mass of jelly.

Cara had disappeared into one of the waiting units when Froggy slid out from under the car, his lipless grin splitting his bland face ear to ear.

"Wonder how come I didn't get a big old hug?" he teased.

"'Cause you were under the car, nitwit." Froggy being one of Holt's best friends, the two traded regular barbs with genuine glee and false disdain.

Froggy sat up, dusting off his palms, back braced against the bumper. "Just as well. Kelly would break my head."

Kelly Priddy, Froggy's doting wife, clearly did not mind her husband's, well, froglike appearance, focusing instead on his good heart. She seemed to think all other women did the same, for she was known for her jealous ways, which Holt had always found rather funny. Suddenly, though, he had a better understanding of Kelly's motivation since he didn't much like the idea of Cara hugging Froggy as she had just hugged him.

"Tell you what we ought to do," Froggy said, getting up off the ground. "We ought to get together, the four of us. Kelly would sure like it, I know."

Holt smiled and agreed, liking the idea. Only later, after Froggy had gone, did it occur to Holt that he had no business even thinking of taking Cara over to the Priddy place as if the two of them were an actual couple. Obviously his feelings for Cara had taken a dangerous path. Whatever she was, whatever the truth of her, she was not for him. He had to rein in these feelings, for nothing could come of them.

Cara had her path to walk, and Holt had his, as ordained by God above. Her path would, Holt suspected, eventually lead her to remarriage and a new father for Ace, but that wouldn't, couldn't, be him. His occupation, his calling, precluded marriage, as Holt knew only too well.

If he didn't feel quite as convinced of that as he once had, he chose not to acknowledge the fact, perhaps because he sensed that doing so could throw his whole world into a tailspin.

* * *

The first full week of February appeared to have been designed to test Holt's limits. The trial started on Sunday, right after church. Before that, Cara had seemed delighted with the world, happier and more relaxed than Holt had yet seen her. Afterward, she turned quiet and sadly contemplative, but none of his gentle prods prompted her to talk to him, and that left him feeling hollow and unappreciated. Then on Monday things really went haywire, starting with a sludge line at the drill site that backed up and gushed filth, blowing sixty feet of pipe out of the hole and missing the drill operator by inches.

The fellow's personal vehicle did not fare so well; a piece of pipe landed on the tailgate of his truck, crumpling it into a vee. Holt saw this as confirmation from God that drilling was no business for a family man, though fully half his crew, the drill operator included, were married with children.

After calling his insurance agent, Holt played plumber until he cleared the clog, wading through hip-deep slag to do it. That required hours of effort and left him so nasty he had to go home to his place to clean up before heading over to the motel.

He arrived later than usual by more than an hour and, to cap his day, found Cara and Ace in Room Five bawling their hearts out.

The sight of Cara sobbing as she jostled and petted her screaming son crushed Holt. He strode across the room, plucked the boy from her grasp and folded her to him with one arm, asking urgently, "What's wrong?"

As Ace sputtered to silence, hiccoughing and gasping, Cara pressed her face to Holt's chest. "I let him fall!"

Holt did a quick inspection of the boy, running his gaze over every visible inch. "Where did he hit?"

Sniffing, Cara reached upward. "His head."

Holt patted her shoulder, feeling paternal and a tad superior in the way of those who manage not to get caught up in a moment of hysteria, never mind how his heart had wrung when he'd come upon them. "Well, he's not bleeding and he's conscious, so it can't be too bad."

As if to confirm this prognosis, Ace sucked in a shuddering breath, laid his head on Holt's shoulder and stuck his hand in his mouth, drooling on Holt's neck.

"It's all my fault!" Cara wailed.

"If I'd been here on time…" Holt began, intending to comfort her, only to lose his train of thought as she clasped her arms around him, butted her face into his chest again and sobbed afresh. Sighing, he caressed the back of her head and let her cry, knowing that all those tears could not really be about a minor childhood accident.

Finally Holt sat her down in the only chair in the room, crouched at her feet with Ace on his knee and pushed away the strands of hair that had slipped from her ponytail. "Okay. Now what is this really about? Ace is fine, but you're making yourself sick over something. What's bothering you?"

She shook her head, not quite meeting his gaze even as she toyed with the edge of his shirt collar.

Holt sighed. "Last week, after we saw Mrs. Poersel, you were jubilant. This week, you're morose. I know something is bothering you, and it started with church yesterday."

In a small voice, she said, "I need to ask you something."

His heart thunked, but he kept his tone level. "Ask away."

Suddenly those soft gray eyes bore into his. "Can God forgive sins that you can't stop doing?"

Rocked, Holt shifted his weight, balancing on his bent toes. "God can forgive any sin that is confessed, Cara, but part of confession is turning away. By confessing our sins we acknowledge we are wrong and turn away from those wrong actions."

She didn't seem too happy with that explanation. "But what if you can't turn away? There are some things you just can't get out of!"

"Like what?"

Lips clamping, she looked toward the door. Ace chose that moment to grab on to Holt's ear and twist it in a bid for his attention. Dredging up every ounce of patience he had left, Holt removed those little fingers with their surprisingly sharp nails from his person. At the same time he addressed Cara.

"You're going to have to trust me at some point, Cara."

That gray gaze zipped right back to his face. "Like you trust me?"

Holt felt as if he'd been kicked, and he didn't like it a bit. His psyche screamed about unfairness and justification. Every suspicion he'd ever had of her came roaring back.

"Give me a way to trust you, Cara," he demanded. "Anything." Questions too long pent up spilled out of him. "Why are your clothes more suited to the tropics than the Pacific Northwest? Why did your lawyer husband leave you destitute? Why were you scared out of your wits to go visit poor old Mrs. Poersel?" Cara turned her head away, silent as a tomb. "Why isn't your brother helping you?" he roared, growing more irate by the moment. "If you were my sister—"

"I'm *not* your sister!" she erupted, shooting up to her feet and sending the chair skittering. "I wish I were! Don't you think I'd rather be your beloved Charlotte than—" She bit her lip.

"What?" he urged, pushing up to his full height and shifting Ace to one side. "Than what, Cara?"

She looked at her son. "Alone," she said, her cracked voice draining away Holt's anger with that one word.

"You and Ace *aren't* alone," Holt vowed.

Taking Ace from him, she slid her hand over the boy's pale head. "I might as well be," she whispered, whirling away. "Maybe it would be better if I was."

Knowing his temper had only made matters worse, Holt let her go.

"You're brooding," Charlotte said, her voice losing none of its censorial tone through the telephone.

Holt didn't argue the point. He could not get his exchange with Cara that afternoon off his mind. In what sin had she trapped herself, and why did she insist on carrying that burden alone? Didn't she know how much he wanted to help her, to trust her? Along with regret for losing his temper came indignation.

She had some nerve, not trusting him, after all he'd done for her.

In light of her stubbornness, he'd begun to think that he had no choice except to use every means at his disposal to figure her out, which was why he'd made this phone call.

"Are you done needling me yet?" he asked his too-perceptive sister. "If so, I'd like to speak to your husband."

Charlotte huffed and passed the telephone to Tyler. Some forty minutes later, Holt had instructions on how to run a detailed computer background check. He'd been careful not to mention Cara's name, which had undoubtedly left his brother-in-law with the impression that his concern centered on one of his roughnecks, but Holt didn't feel nearly as bad about that as he did about needing to find answers for the puzzle that was Cara.

Still, he dithered, torn between his need to know and his fear of knowing.

By morning, he'd all but convinced himself not to go through with it. Then, an hour or so before lunch, an overwhelming urge seized him. He left the rig site and drove straight to the motel. As expected, Hap and his cronies played Forty-Two at the table in the front room while Ace napped peacefully in the apartment and Cara tended to her work, leaving Holt free to slip behind the counter, retrieve Cara's employment file and seat himself in front of the computer in the office.

Holt didn't know exactly what he hoped to accomplish, but when Ty had told him how to use a popular satellite imaging site to check out physical addresses, he'd thought about how much relief he'd felt after stopping by Cara's old address in Duncan. Perhaps checking out Cara's previous address in Oregon this way would also ease his doubts.

Thanks to the lightning-fast Internet connection, Holt located the necessary Web site within moments. He typed in the address and sat in amazement as the satellite beamed onto his screen an actual aerial photo of the site. He couldn't tell too much about it until he figured out how to zoom in, and then his hopes plummeted. Just in case he'd gotten something wrong, he went through the whole process again several times from step one, but no matter what he did that same image kept loading onto the computer screen.

For some minutes he sat there staring at the used car lot where Cara Jane Wynne had supposedly lived until widowed less than a year earlier. Clearly it had been decades, at best, since any residential structure could have stood at that address.

Sick at heart, Holt rubbed a hand across his forehead, trying to think of every possible reason why Cara might have found it necessary to use a bogus address. Suddenly he remembered making a photocopy of her driver's license. Flipping through her folder, he found the photocopy. Would the state of Oregon have issued a license with an incorrect address? Not likely.

Hands shaking, Holt looked up the Social Security number

in her file, then went to the Web site that Ty had recommended. It took several tries for him to get the data that he sought, but when the necessary page finally loaded, he carefully read the information provided, information corresponding to the number that Cara had repeatedly written on her employment forms.

That number did, indeed, belong to Cara Jane Wynne. Unfortunately the Cara Jane Wynne to whom that number belonged had been born in 1926!

Holt dropped his head into his hands, close to tears and intending to pray, but his mind seemed frozen to the fact that the woman he knew as Cara Jane Sharp Wynne had assumed a false identity. The most logical explanation seemed to be that she'd assumed the identity of her late aunt. How else would Cara have known Mrs. Poersel? Holt realized that she'd used that knowledge to consolidate her position at the Heavenly Arms, and a tide of all-too-familiar anger swamped him. Before he even knew it, he was on his feet and striding for the door, intent on confrontation.

Hap, Grover and the others stopped what they were doing to watch him leave, but Holt said not a word. What could he say? That he'd known all along she was a liar? That he could have proven it weeks ago if he'd just had the nerve? That he'd somehow let himself drift in an agony of attraction and doubt?

He caught her preparing to enter one of the rooms. The smile with which she greeted him cut him to the quick, and that just ratcheted up his temper another notch. Striking a pose, he brought his hands to his hips, one knee cocked.

"So you lived at a used car lot," he accused without preamble. He'd intended to use a light, ironic tone but had been unable to prevent a sarcastic edge.

The color drained from her face, telling him that she hadn't just pulled that address out of thin air. She'd picked it on purpose. He tried to laugh.

"Guess there could've been a house there once, say forty years ago. But no problem, right, since you were born in 1926!"

She literally reeled, bouncing off the building at her back. He hadn't meant to shout. He'd meant to be as cold as steel, but his voice had risen out of control.

"Why, Cara?" he demanded. "Or is that even your name?"

She nodded mutely, and that he felt even the slightest relief infuriated him all over again.

"Where did you get the false ID?" he demanded, wanting her to understand that this went beyond mere lies.

At least she didn't deny it. "A-a man my h-husband knew."

"You've broken the law. You get that, don't you?"

"Y-yes," came her only answer. She glanced up at him then, her gray eyes wide and stark in her pale face.

Surprisingly, in the face of such woe and despondence, he found it difficult to hold on to his anger, but he couldn't just let it go. "Is that all you've got to say for yourself?"

Shaking her head, she croaked, "I'll clear out."

She left the housekeeping cart where it stood and stumbled away, hands clasped before her, shoulders hunched. He watched her go, his justifiable anger sliding into extreme frustration.

"Arrrrgh!"

Grasping tufts of hair with both hands, he waited. It was over. He'd proved her a liar, and that was the end of it.

Yet, the much-hoped-for relief did not materialize. Instead, frustration quickly morphed into dismay and then, suddenly, something very like panic.

Throwing back his head, he gazed heavenward, reaching out in wordless agony for understanding, enlightenment. When it came, he'd have rejected it if he could have, but truth was truth, and the awful truth was that he did not want her to go, could not let it be over.

He wanted her to stay. Even more than that, he wanted the truth, he wanted her to stay.

Bowing his head, he pressed the heels of his hands to his eyes and spoke urgently to God in his mind.

Now what? The lies are out there, and I'm still lost. Help me. Show me what to do. You've never failed me yet, Lord. Show me how to let her go. Or how to make her stay.

Swallowing, he started for her room.

She threw her clothing on the bed, mostly because in her urgency and terror she couldn't remember what she'd done with the suitcases. She had to get out of there fast, before she came apart or Holt notified the authorities. She couldn't take time to cry, to plan, to think. She had to go. Now.

Of course she'd known that it would come to this. For a little while after her visit with Mrs. Poersel, she'd lived in the happy dream of everything being okay, of her lies going undetected and Holt's suspicions of her dwindling into forgotten impulse. She'd gone to church on Sunday morning convinced that the worst lay behind her. Then Grover had spoken from the tenth chapter of Romans, sweeping away her relief and hope in the space of a few minutes.

Not only did the lies and secrets still exist, Cara had seen that they literally held her captive and would eventually destroy her.

Now they had. Or soon would if she didn't get out of there.

Closing an empty dresser drawer, she hurried into the closet and grabbed her son's things off the shelf, remembering only then that Ace slept in the apartment across the way. Panicked, she tossed his stuff at the bed and rushed toward the door, only to draw up short when it opened and Holt strode into the room.

He took one look at the bed, closed the door and leaned against it. "Stop it."

Steeling herself, she lunged forward and tried to push him out of the way. "I have to get my son!"

"Stop it!" he commanded again, refusing to budge. "I only want to help." Seizing her by the upper arms, he shook her hard enough to snap her head back. "Don't you get it? I want to help."

She tried to push his hands away, teetering on the very edge of control. "You can't help! No one can. I have to do it myself. That's my only chance!"

"For what?" he demanded.

"To protect my son!"

She clapped a hand over her mouth, lest the whole ugly story fall out.

"From who? From what?" he pleaded, olive-green gaze darkened with concern and something else she'd rather not identify.

"I can't tell you." Too late she realized that his anger could be borne easier than his pain and disappointment, much easier than his caring. She shook her head, forced back the tears, and shut her eyes so she wouldn't have to see the emotion in his.

"Answer me one question," he begged, dropping his hands from her. "Are you hiding from Ace's father?"

"No! No. My husband is dead."

Until she saw Holt's relief, she didn't even realize that she'd looked at him. She slammed her eyes shut again when he reached for her. As his long, strong arms folded her against him, she cried out, afraid she might shatter. For a long moment, she tried to resist his comfort and the hope it offered, but both lures proved too great. She gave up and leaned into him, weak with need.

His large, capable hand invaded her hair, pressing her head against his chest. Listening to the beat of his heart, letting the heat of his body warm her chilled, raw nerve endings, she absorbed him, from his unique, earthy scent to the strength that defined him. In that moment nothing had ever seemed more dear, more sweet, more safe.

Knowledge coalesced. She understood in a blinding flash that she had misjudged him. Holt was not like any other man she'd known, not her absent, ghostlike father, not her scheming, selfish brother, not her arrogant, egotistical father-in-law, not her shallow, self-absorbed husband. Especially not her late husband.

Addison had never argued with her about anything; neither had he consulted her, even about her own likes and dislikes, which he had ignored as blithely as he'd discounted her concerns and hurts. She'd often wondered if she mattered to him as much as his stylish wardrobe and luxury car. He'd seemed to consider her nothing more than a convenience, an adjunct to his home, which hadn't really even been his but simply a way for his parents to keep their only son dancing to their tune.

No, Holt wasn't anything like Addison. Not only did Holt make his own way in the world, he did it without cutting corners and worked to assure everyone in his orbit the same privilege. Including her.

What was it then that disturbed her so greatly about Holt? Something more than just the fear that he would feel morally bound to inform her in-laws of her whereabouts colored her reactions to this man.

She had her answer a moment later when he tugged her head back and kissed her.

Until that very instant, she hadn't realized how long she'd been waiting for him to do that. When she found herself looping her arms about his neck, she understood how ardently she wanted this, how keenly she had hoped for it. Only then, as sweetness poured into her and her foolish heart sang, did she admit to herself that the problem wasn't Holt at all.

The problem was how she felt about him.

Chapter Thirteen

In the end she stayed simply because Holt asked it of her.

"We need you around here, Cara, in case you haven't noticed."

"I want to stay," she admitted shakily, not quite able to look at him after that kiss. "Just don't ask me questions that I can't answer, Holt, please." She didn't know how he'd found out that she'd faked her identity, but it hardly mattered. The only surprise, really, was that it had taken him so long.

She sat on the edge of the bed amid the strewn clothing and gazed determinedly at her hands. Holt stood beside the door, poised to exit, as if the need to touch might seize them both again unawares. She appreciated the distance and lamented it at the same time.

"Will you tell me your real name, at least?"

"No." Then, because she somehow needed him to know, she relented as far as she was able. "Cara Kay. Cara Kay Sharp. I won't give you my married name. Don't ask."

"Not Cara Jane then," he commented in a rueful voice.

"Cara Jane was my great-aunt," she told him, figuring he already knew. "I think I hoped by taking her full name to keep the best part of my old life and maybe even to be something like her."

"A good woman, then."

"The best I've ever known."

"Mrs. Poersel certainly seemed fond of her."

"They were very close."

"She raised you," he ventured cautiously. "Your aunt raised you?"

"Yes." Cara winced, finding it very difficult to lie to him. "And no. She was a great influence on my life, but I only spent summers with her. From as far back as I can remember until she died."

"Ah. That explains a lot." He rubbed a hand over his face, seeming weary and frazzled.

"You have to understand," she pleaded, gazing up at Holt. "Those were the best times of my childhood. They're all that got me through the rest of it. Aunt Jane sent the bus tickets, knowing my mother was always glad to get rid of us. Mom had to keep us during the school year. Otherwise she couldn't get the food stamps and other assistance, but in the summer we were Aunt Jane's. I always thought of it as going home to my real life."

His gaze seemed to turn inward. "You clung to the place and times when it all felt good, didn't you? That's why you came back to Oklahoma."

She nodded, slumping forward with relief. She had wondered if he could understand, given the caliber of his own family. Yes, he'd suffered loss and tragedy, but he'd had Hap and Ryan and Charlotte and even this whole town.

Eden, indeed. She wondered if he knew how clean and whole and safe and entirely beautiful this place seemed to her, with its ever-present pump jacks sucking the black oil from the earth, its streets named for trees and flowers and the park with its grand, whimsical bridge spanning a narrow, muddy stream. The three blocks of downtown, with its circa 1930s storefronts, felt like an oasis to her, an immutable place in a world of constant change. Why, the most modern building in town seemed to be the little city hall at the north end of Garden Avenue, but she hadn't seen the schools or any points east of Booker's old-fashioned grocery. Old buildings were not what gave the town its sense of community, however. That came from its friendly people. What she wouldn't give to be a real part of a town like this.

"I didn't want to lie to you," she told Holt in a small, wavering voice. "I don't want to keep secrets. I'm so sorry."

He opened the door a crack and stood staring through it for some moments before he faced her again. "Give me the driver's license and Social Security card so I can destroy them."

She would be trapped then. Oh, she could still run if she had to, but how would she find work? How would she support Ace?

"Give them to me, Cara," he repeated softly. "It has to end here."

Without further thought, she went to the bedside table and drew out her wallet, including every dollar of her savings, from the drawer. She handed over the whole thing and waited while he thumbed through it, extracted the cards and slipped them into his hip pocket before passing the wallet back to her. She snapped it closed and folded her arms.

He opened the door a little wider. "All right," he said, just that and nothing more. Then he left her.

Cara fell onto the bed, weak with emotion. She did not know what would happen next. She had placed herself and her son in Holt Jefford's large, capable hands. Now she could only pray that it had been the wisest course. But really, with her heart telling her to stay and nowhere else to go, what else could she have done?

When she finally dragged herself back to work, Holt had gone, and he did not return to help her that afternoon or any that followed for the rest of the week. Accepting Holt's absence as far less than she deserved, Cara left Ace to Hap's tender care in the afternoons and went about her business as best she could.

All else remained as it had been, with Holt and often Ryan dragging in to plant their feet beneath the dinner table, except that Holt would take himself off again as soon as he finished his meal, and Cara would pretend that her heart did not go with him.

Obviously he had said nothing to Hap or anyone else about what he'd learned, and for that she felt profound, if silent, gratitude. Just one question plagued her.

How long, she wondered, could it go on? How long before one of them broke beneath the strain?

"Hel-lo-o!"

That single word called out from the kitchen galvanized the entire dinner table. Three forks dropped and three chairs scooted back at the same time.

"My stars!" exclaimed Hap, as everyone got their feet. "It's Charlotte!"

A slight redhead appeared in the doorway just as Ryan, whose chair stood closest to the kitchen, reached it.

"Sis!"

Grabbing her up in a bear hug, he spun with her in his arms. Charlotte Jefford Aldrich laughed, then launched herself at Holt, who caught her as easily as he might have done Ace. With much laughter, he sat her on her feet. She turned with outstretched arms to Hap.

"Granddad."

The old man's chin wobbled, which was all it took to make Cara's eyes water. She'd been living on the edge of tears ever since Holt had learned of her duplicity.

After a long hug, Hap backed away, rasping, "You look fine. Marriage agrees with you."

Beaming, Charlotte took hold of the sides of her fine, brown tweed jacket, holding them out as she might a skirt, and turned in a circle, showing off expensive jeans and a rust-colored cashmere turtleneck that perfectly matched the lining of the jacket. Cara wouldn't have been surprised to see her decked out in satin and furs, given what she'd heard about the Aldrich fortune.

"Where's Ty?" Ryan asked, looking past Charlotte expectantly.

"Putting our luggage in our room. Assuming it's empty and our key still works."

Hap snorted at that. He usually kept the room vacant just for them. He turned to Cara, waving a hand. "Charlotte, honey, this here is Cara Jane and her boy, Ace. We told you about her."

Cringing inwardly at Hap's use of her aunt's full name, Cara rose as Charlotte reached a hand across the table, a smile warming her pleasant face. "Hello, Cara Ja—"

"Just Cara, please," she interrupted. Cara Jane seemed so false now, a constant reminder of her dishonesty.

"It's nice to meet you, Cara. I've heard so much about you and your son. All good."

That made Cara want to cry again, but she just smiled weakly and returned the compliment. "Oh, it couldn't be as good as what your brothers and grandfather have to say about you and your husband."

Charlotte laughed and squeezed her hand. "My family's prejudiced in that regard." She swept her gaze over the table, lifting her eyebrows at the chicken enchilada casserole and salad that Cara had made for Friday dinner. "This looks good. Is there enough for two more?"

"There is if Holt don't make his usual hog of himself," Hap declared, sitting down.

Holt rolled his eyes, going for extra chairs, while Ryan dipped into the kitchen for more plates and cutlery. "Why does everybody pick on my eating habits?"

"Maybe because we all envy you," said a newcomer, striding into the room. This had to be Tyler Aldrich, Charlotte's husband. Handsome in a bland, well-groomed way with dark hair and pale blue eyes, he beamed at the assembled group.

Hap came to his feet again. Tyler engulfed the old man in an affectionate hug and kissed him on the cheek. Holt hurried over to drop the chairs and pump Tyler's hand, while Ryan all but threw the plates onto the table in order to be next while Hap introduced Cara and Ace. Everyone sat down, rearranging to make room for the couple. Somehow Holt wound up sitting next to Cara, his arm balanced on the upper back edge of her chair.

Charlotte dished out meals for Ty and herself amid a babble of conversation concerning their unexpected arrival and Ty's mother's health.

"We thought we'd surprise you, that's all," Charlotte said.

"Mom's fine," Tyler supplied. "Scared us a bit until we figured out the problem."

"Ty's sister is looking out for her while we're gone," Charlotte added.

Ty looked at Holt meaningfully. "You wouldn't believe how those three women gang up on me. I cannot wait to get our house built here, even if my brother is threatening to move in with us to escape Mom and sis. Speaking of which, I have the blueprints in my car."

That launched the men into the subject of building. Charlotte, meanwhile, confided to Cara, "He doesn't mean a word of it. He adores his family."

Tyler pressed a kiss to her temple. "Especially you." He went back to his discussion, forking up bites of chicken enchilada between comments. Ty sat back, apparently replete, and turned his attention to Cara. "That was very good. Thank you."

Charlotte nodded, smiling. "I think I'll be needing this recipe."

"We'll trade then," Cara told her. "These guys are always asking for things I've never heard of before. What, by the way, is chicken and dumplings?"

"Chicken stewed with onions and a kind of batter that makes a rich sauce and thick lumps called dumplings," Charlotte explained. "I put peas in mine."

"Black-eyed peas again," Cara muttered. Hap and Holt erupted in laughter.

"It's green peas," Charlotte clarified, "but what is this about black-eyed peas?"

Hap waved a hand. "Cara just happened to join us on New Year's Eve."

Charlotte dropped her fork. "And no doubt you made the poor girl cook that very night!"

"Believe me, it was better than the alternative," Cara said. She flushed red the next instant. Thankfully both Holt and Hap laughed again, agreeing heartily, but that did little to ameliorate her embarrassment. "I'll, um, just clear the table and start the dishes," she muttered, reaching for soiled plates.

"I'll help," Holt announced, rising.

"That's my job," Ryan protested lightly from his chair.

Cara rose, shaking her head. "No, no. You two enjoy your visit with your sister. If you'll just watch Ace for a few minutes, I can make quick work of these."

"I'll help you," Holt said firmly, taking the stacked plates from her hands.

Charlotte and Ty traded looks. Then a smile spread across Ty's face. "Lots to be said for doing dishes," he told Holt meaningfully.

"You would know," Holt retorted, carrying the plates into the kitchen.

Cara slid a puzzled glance around the table, took in the speculative expressions, put her head down and snatched up as many dirty dishes as she could carry before hurrying out after Holt. She found him leaning back against the counter, his big hands cupping its rolled edge. Only after she'd put in the stopper and started the water running did Holt speak.

"Ty used to wash dishes just so he could be close to Charlotte," he informed her.

Cara's heart thunked. "Oh." No one had to tell her that Holt's motives differed in regard to herself.

In confirmation of that fact, Holt softly said, "I just thought I ought to tell you not to bother servicing Number Eight while Charlotte and Ty are here. Like most newlyweds, they value their privacy."

Cara nodded and willed away her envy. "I understand."

As she squirted soap into the stream of running water, Holt reached beneath the sink for the scrap can, crowding close. She skittered out of his way, gasping, "What are you doing?"

He turned a frown up at her. "Helping clean up."

Cara looked at the pile of dirty dishes on the counter and shook her head. It hurt to know that he'd used this just as an excuse to caution her about maintaining the privacy of the newlyweds. No one had to tell her that he regretted that kiss. His absences had spoken volumes on that score.

"I—I'd rather you tended to Ace. He's missed you." She felt lower than an inchworm, using her son to get rid of Holt, even if what she'd said happened to be true.

Holt stared at her before plunking down the can on the counter and leaving the room. A moment later, she heard him exclaim, "Hey, little buddy, come along with me."

She knew that he took Ace from his makeshift high chair

and carried him into the outer room. The others soon followed, though Charlotte first popped in to offer assistance.

"Oh, no. This is what I'm paid to do," Cara protested. "Besides, your family's anxious to spend time with you." After a pause, Charlotte smiled, nodded and left her.

Alone in the kitchen, it felt to Cara as if she'd lost her own place in the family, which was absurd. She'd never had a place in the Jefford family. No matter how kind the Jeffords had been, she was hired help, just as she'd told Charlotte, and that position was precarious at best.

With that in mind, as soon as Cara finished cleaning, she went to fetch her son, declaring, "Bath time."

Ace stood on Holt's feet, giggling happily, his tiny hands lost in Holt's much larger ones, while Holt moved his knees up and down, pretending to march from a sitting position on the couch. Cara picked up her son, grasping him just beneath his arms. To her chagrin, as she lifted him, the boy made a grab for Holt, one hand closing in the fabric of Holt's shirt.

"You've got a fan there," Tyler commented laconically, sitting next to Charlotte on the opposite couch, his arm about her shoulders.

"Yeah, we're real buddies," Holt said as Cara pried Ace loose.

He screeched as Cara swiftly carried him away from Holt. Nodding blind smiles in the direction of Charlotte and Tyler, Cara moved for the door, calling out, "Nice to meet you."

The usual, polite rejoinders followed her from the room. Holt did not. She didn't expect him to, which made her disappointment that much more difficult to explain.

Cara woke the next morning to the sound of something hitting the window. When she opened the door, what peppered her face felt cold and wet. She turned on the television to find a weather alert crawling across the bottom of the screen.

The long-predicted weather front had finally arrived, dumping sleet over New Mexico, Texas and Oklahoma. Authorities advised everyone to stay indoors and off the roads, but how many would have missed or ignored that warning? Cara looked out the window, unsurprised to find a strange car parked beneath the drive-through. It wouldn't be the last vehicle to stop at the motel that day.

Over the course of a few hours, sleet turned the roads and ground into one giant skating rink. Icicles grew from eaves and tree branches, tinkling like wind chimes in the frosty breeze. It soon became obvious that they had a real crisis brewing.

Before lunchtime, half a dozen other vehicles slid, literally, into the lot, two of them winding up in the ditch alongside the roadway. By early afternoon, tractor trailer rigs lined the road, leaving barely a single lane free for travel, had anything been moving. Those without sleeper compartments wanted rooms in which to wait out the storm. Fortunately, many of the regular oil field workers who bunked weekdays at the Heavenly Arms had set out the evening before for their respective homes, leaving some of the rooms contracted by the local oil companies free for rental. Those who'd slept in found themselves as stuck as everyone else.

"We'll have 'em stacked up like cordwood if this don't let up," Hap worried.

He sent Cara out to ask the remaining oil field workers to double up, freeing more space. Not ten minutes after she returned to the lobby, Holt showed up with a family of six.

"Found them stranded in their car behind a sand truck," he explained. The county vehicle had broken down right in the middle of the highway. "They've got someone out there working on it now, but I'm betting 81 is blocked for at least tonight."

Hap looked at the bedraggled couple and their four children, all elementary age or older, standing in the warmth of the lobby. "They can use Cara's room, but we don't have any more cots. Won't be enough beds."

"Or blankets," Charlotte added, coming in from the apartment. They'd all been scrambling to accommodate the refugees from the storm, but Charlotte had been a one-woman army, in constant motion with her auburn braid flying out behind her. "I've called Ryan on my cell," she reported, "and he'll take these folks over at his place if Holt can get them there."

Holt nodded. "What I don't know is whether or not I can get back out to my place. Took me all day to get into town, and the roads are worse now than when I started out."

"What I'm wondering," Tyler said, arriving just then, "is how we're going to feed this lot."

Hap whistled. "I'll call Teddy and Grover. Maybe they'll have some ideas."

"I'll get our things moved over here," Cara said.

"Good idea," Holt told her, nodding toward the front window. A man bundled against the cold tramped and slid on foot across the lawn. "Looks like we'll be needing it."

"Tyler and I can sleep in here," Charlotte volunteered, nodding toward the lobby, "so Cara and Ace can have my old room."

"Naw, you can have my bed," Hap said. "I'll sleep on one of the couches."

"I'm going to need the other," Holt informed them all. "For now, let's just get these folks over to Ryan's and everyone else moved. If we have to, we'll make other adjustments later."

The man pushed through the outer door just then, gasping and looking worried. "Can you put up two kids and two adults? My family's stuck in our car maybe a mile up the road."

Holt looked at Hap before addressing the harried fellow. "You come along with me." He nodded toward the family of six. "We'll drop off these folks, pick up your bunch, and the room will be ready when we get back."

The fellow closed his eyes in relief. "Thank you. Thank you."

"Thank God for snow chains," Holt said, going through the door.

"Where on earth did he get snow chains?" Tyler wondered aloud, as the party filed out.

"Eh, he keeps 'em in case he has to check on his rig and crew out in the panhandle," Hap explained. "They get lots worse weather out there than we do here. Usually."

Charlotte looked to Cara. "I'll help you move your things. Ty will take care of ours."

"Me and Ace will hold down the fort here," Hap said, waving them away.

Tyler had been spreading rock salt, which made walking across the pavement a little easier. Instead of hauling everything across to the apartment, however, Cara decided to take just what they'd need most and leave the rest in the trunk of her car, mindful of the cramped conditions in Charlotte's old room. With Charlotte's help, it didn't take long. Cara made a stoic, silent vow not to care, though it felt as if she'd lost her one true sanctuary.

"I'll come back and change the sheets," Cara said as they left, their arms full.

"I'll get the laundry started then," Charlotte said, "but I don't think we ought to be worrying about housekeeping until the roads clear. Folks can do for themselves until this passes."

"Now we just have to figure out how to feed everyone."

"Oh, I wouldn't worry about that," Charlotte told her with a smile.

Within the hour, Grover and Teddy showed up on foot with bags of groceries and the news that both Booker's store and the café downtown had opened and would remain so as long as necessary. Moreover, city workers were busy sanding and salting. The highways and county roads remained closed, but the city would soon be maneuverable, at least in the short-term, with more sleet predicted during the night.

Thanking God that she and Ace were safe from the storm, along with everyone else at the motel, Cara promised herself that would be enough for her. More, surely, than she deserved.

Chapter Fourteen

Outside, streetlamps softly illuminated a sparkling wonderland of trees, grass and buildings frosted in ice. Inside, with everyone hunkered down for the night, the Jeffords figured they might as well enjoy their time together. Despite predictions of more sleet and frigid temperatures, everyone could relax and wait out the storm.

The family sat down to a meal prepared by Cara and Charlotte. Hap spoke an eloquent prayer of thanksgiving and petition over it. Afterward, Hap smiled at those around the table.

"We couldn't have got through this day without every one of you."

Cara smiled. She'd felt very much a part of things all day long. They'd worked together side by side to handle the crisis, not just the Jeffords but the whole town.

They spent the evening playing dominoes and watching weather reports on the TV. To Cara's surprise and secret pleasure, Holt took it upon himself to teach her the game of Forty-Two, pulling her chair close to his and murmuring instructions in her ear. Laughter and a sense of well-being blanketed them all as surely as ice blanketed the ground outside. Nevertheless, Cara tried to maintain an emotional distance.

She dared not believe that, just because Holt knew some of her secrets and hadn't turned out her and her son, all would be well. The worst, to her shame, remained hidden and must continue that way. With that in mind, Cara and Ace retired for the night before everyone else.

The day's activity should have guaranteed both a sound night's sleep. Unfortunately, neither rested well. Ace had gotten too acclimated to the portable crib, now being used by a three-year-old in Room 12, and Cara could not completely relax for fear that Ace would roll off the side of the high double bed that they shared.

Morning found her bleary and aching, but the hot coffee and breakfast that Charlotte provided helped. Though reluctant—attending services these days just seemed to depress her—Cara got ready and tramped with everyone else across the lawn and up the street to the church. Normal Sunday dress yielded to necessity, which left her decked out in jeans, a sweater of Charlotte's, Hap's old coat and a pair of galoshes. The condition of the outlying roads naturally diminished the congregation, but nothing diminished the agony of guilt that Cara continued to carry in her heart, and as usual Holt noticed.

"You okay?" he asked quietly, trudging along beside her on the way back to the motel after the service. He carried Ace, as he had earlier.

Cara nodded, determined to feel only gratitude. "Yes, thank you."

"Are you two comfortable in Charlotte's old room?"

"We'll manage," she said, before succumbing to concern. "Although, I'd appreciate if someone could push the bed up against the dresser so Ace can't fall off it. Otherwise I don't know how I can put him down for a nap."

"I'll see to it after lunch," Holt promised.

He shifted the bed, with Tyler's help, as soon as they rose from the luncheon table. Charlotte, however, saw the real problem.

"We've got to clean this out," she decided. "I shouldn't have put it off this long."

"Oh, no. It's all right," Cara protested, "so long as Ace can't fall out of bed."

Charlotte wouldn't let it rest, however, bringing up the subject over breakfast the next morning. "There's just no good excuse," she stated flatly, "and it's not like we have anything else to do today."

"But it's a lot of trouble," Cara pointed out, "for temporary convenience." She'd thought about it during the night and decided that she couldn't, in good conscience, go on taking up rentable space, no matter how much it hurt to relinquish that little kitchenette, if Charlotte insisted on cleaning out her old bedroom. "So if you're sure about this, then Ace and I will make the move permanent."

Holt got up from the table and walked over to gaze into the bedroom, rubbing his chin. "I've got a smaller bedroom set at my place," he said. "We could swap them out. That would help a lot. Provided you girls approve."

"It's Cara's call," Charlotte insisted. "Maybe by the time we get all this junk emptied out, the roads will be clear enough for the two of you to go take a look at it." Abruptly, she snapped her fingers. "I wonder if Agnes Dilberry's still got that crib for sale."

"I'll find out," Holt said.

"Me and Ace are gonna watch the reports," Hap announced, hobbling toward the front room. "One of you bring him out to me."

Holt strode over and plucked the boy from his seat, following Hap.

"Granddad sure is fond of that little guy," Charlotte said, leaning her elbows on the table.

"I'm glad of that," Cara admitted.

"Not as fond as Holt, though," Charlotte went on. "I thought Ryan was the one with an affinity for children, but you two seem to have worked a change in my big brother."

Cara muttered, "Oh, I don't think it's anything we've done."

Charlotte chuckled and confided softly, "It's not just Ace. He follows you with his eyes every moment. Hardly even tries to hide it."

He's probably afraid I'll steal something, Cara remarked to herself, bowing her head.

Holt reappeared just then, his cell phone in hand. "I called Agnes. She'll have the crib ready for pickup soon as the weather clears."

"Oh. Uh, I don't know," Cara began, thinking of her meager savings. "How much does she want for it?"

"Why?" Holt asked. "You're not paying for it."

"But—"

"I'll let the two of you work it out," Charlotte said airily, popping up and moving toward the bedroom. "Just remember, big brother, you catch more flies with honey than acid."

Holt stared down at Cara. "I'm not trying to catch flies."

"Girlfriends, then!" came the retort from the bedroom.

Holt's gaze never wavered from Cara's.

Blinking rapidly, she opened her mouth to speak, but what was she supposed to say in light of his silence? After a moment, he followed his sister into the bedroom.

Cara felt stuck to the chair.

Why, she wondered, hadn't he spoken up? Why let his sister assume that they were linked romantically? Holt simply could not think of her that way, despite that one kiss, not now that he knew what he did about her. Could he?

* * *

Ridiculous! Holt told himself as the knot in his stomach tightened. What did it matter what Cara thought of his place? He'd proudly built the house nearly ten years ago, and he loved living out here in the middle of this quarter section, surrounded by his own land and his own cattle and his own things. He didn't care what anyone else thought of it. Except suddenly he did.

He took the turn off the narrow county road, the truck bumping roughly over the cattle guard. Beside him, Cara sat up a little straighter, her gaze avidly sweeping the area.

"Oh, this is wonderful," she said, but he imagined her comment had to do with being out and about after three days cooped up inside the motel. "I love the trees and the way the ground sort of rolls, even the barn. It's beautiful."

Holt relaxed somewhat as the truck barreled down the long, dusty drive. Okay, so she didn't hate the surroundings, not that it mattered. He was *not* trying to impress her. He didn't know what he was doing with her, frankly, only that he hated the air of shame and timidity about her lately. He ached for her sometimes, but he didn't have a clue what to do to help her. She'd lied, bought fake identity papers from some creep that her husband had known and wouldn't reveal why, even when confronted, but Holt had come to the conclusion that it must be for a good reason. He couldn't reconcile anything else with the woman and mother he'd found her to be, and he was sick and tired of trying to keep a "safe" distance between them.

The truck made the curve in the drive, and she gasped.

"You built this? All by yourself?"

He brought the truck to a stop in its usual spot beneath the carport and killed the engine. "Who told you?"

"Charlotte," she answered, opening her door with one hand and releasing her safety belt with the other.

A gust of wind whipped through the brief opening. Thanks to that dry wind every exposed expanse of road had been swept clean during the night, despite the frigid temperatures. Holt hurried to join Cara on the porch, where she huddled inside Hap's old coat, one mittened hand placed flat against the paneled door.

"Red!" she exclaimed approvingly.

"To match the roof and the barn," he admitted, reaching down to turn the knob and get them both out of that cruel wind. He'd never seen the need to lock up the place out here.

Her eyes wide, Cara tiptoed through the tiny foyer set off by spindles from the greater room. Head pivoting, she took in everything from the open living area with its spare leather furniture to the kitchen visible beyond the L-shaped breakfast bar and the empty dining space.

"I especially like the floor," she said.

Holt had laid every plank of the polished wood by his own hand. "Charlotte picked out the rugs," he told her, puffed up with pride.

Cara looked at the bandanna-patterned throw rugs. "I see you love red." He shrugged, inordinately pleased that she'd pegged his favorite color.

"How many bedrooms?" she asked.

"Two." He gestured toward the hallway branching off on his right. "And two baths." He pointed to a door in the back wall of the kitchen. "Laundry room's over there, and that…" He directed his finger to the glass-paned door off one end of the living area. "That's my office."

He knew the place must seem somewhat bare to her, especially when compared to Hap's apartment, but Holt found it easier to keep the place neat and clean that way.

"It must be wonderful to own your own home," she commented wistfully, "and to be able to do this all yourself." She spread her hands. "Amazing."

Holt bowed his head, smiling as much at his earlier nervousness as at her approval of his home. "Thanks," he said, adding quickly, "The bedroom set we could swap for is in here." As he led her down the hall to a door on the left, he asked casually, "You and your husband didn't own a house then?"

"We lived in a house," she said. "It wasn't ours, though. It belonged to my in-laws." He paused, and she leaned a shoulder against the cream-colored wall, smiling ruefully. "Decorated and maintained according to their dictates."

Holt raised his eyebrows at that. "But it was your home even if it was their house."

She shook her head. "Not really. Whatever they thought we should have, that's what we had. Whatever they thought we should do, that's what we did. What *he* did." She dropped her gaze, murmuring, "They're very controlling. I should have realized they held the deed to the house."

Holt goggled at that. "You didn't know?"

"Not until Addison died," she told him, folding her arms.

"Your husband didn't tell you that your house belonged to his parents?" Holt couldn't believe the subject hadn't come up between them at some point.

"Addison wouldn't have," she answered softly, "because he knew what it meant to me." She lifted her head then, explaining, "You see, my brother and I grew up in apartments, a whole string of them, each one more of a dump than the last." A wan smile curled her lips. "I thought Aunt Jane's old house was a palace until I married Addison. Then I found out that luxury does not make a home." She pushed away from the wall, saying, "If you must know, that little kitchenette at the motel is the closest I've ever come to actually having a home of my own."

"Then you shouldn't give it up," Holt stated, hating that she'd done so even temporarily.

She shook her head, smiling. "No, it's best this way. It will be easier all around, for Ace especially. Besides," she added, "it feels more like we—" Breaking off, she looked away.

"Belong," he said, finding the word only as he said it. She nodded, keeping her gaze averted. *Maybe that's because you do,* he thought. Waving a hand, he silently invited her to take a look inside the room.

She stuck her head in, looking over the sleek furniture. "This is nice stuff. Are you sure you want to give it up?"

"I don't ever use it. Besides, Charlotte's old furniture is much finer. It's just bigger and more ornate than my usual style."

Cara shot him a shy smile. "I think I prefer your style."

"Okay. We'll swap it out then."

Her glowing smile was all the thanks he needed, enough to tell him that he'd been kidding himself long enough. The time had come to face facts. He still didn't know if anything could or should come of them, but he could no longer deny that his feelings were fully engaged.

He knew that he would be spending long hours in earnest prayer about that, leaving it to God how it all ultimately played out. He could only hope that, when all had been said and done, no one would be the worse for it.

Charlotte and Ty took their leave on Wednesday, the day before Valentine's Day. Cara and Ace settled into the apartment, his new crib tucked into a corner of the bedroom. A high chair and baby monitor had been acquired from the Dilberry attic, as well the fine oak crib. Cara felt almost like a part of the family, but that did not prepare her for what she found when she walked out of the bedroom the next afternoon with a newly awakened Ace in her arms.

Holt and Hap stood shoulder to shoulder, the former in his

Sunday best, the other holding a mixed bouquet of flowers and a huge, heart-shaped box of chocolates.

"Happy Valentine's Day," Holt said. Cara promptly burst into laughing tears.

"Couldn't let the day go by unnoticed," Hap rasped, handing over the goodies. "Now go get yourself changed. Holt's taking you out on the town."

"Oh, but—"

"Grover and Marie are coming over with dinner, so don't be worrying none about me and the boy," Hap insisted.

"Charlotte left something in the closet for you," Holt told her. While Cara stood with her mouth open, he took Ace from her, adding, "And by 'town,' Hap means Lawton."

"That's fifty miles away!"

"So we'd best get an early start." With that, he turned her by the shoulder and gave her a little shove. Cara dithered for a moment, but then she rushed back into her room, excitement filling her. To think that they'd all done this for her! Hurrying to the closet, she found the garment bag hanging from the rod. She'd wondered why that had been left in there but had assumed that it contained some memento of Charlotte's. Opening the bag, she found a long-sleeved black velour knit dress with a square neckline and a pair of black velvet mules with kitten heels.

Blessing Charlotte for her generosity, Cara threw off her own clothes and went to work. Twenty minutes later, she stepped out of the bedroom, her heart pounding. With the use of a rubber band and a few pins, she'd managed to put up her hair in a simple twist with a spray of wisps coming out the top. Her plain, gold hoop earrings and a small pendant added a touch of glamour. Because she was shorter than Charlotte, the sleeves of the dress puddled at her wrists and the slightly flared skirt reached almost to her ankles, but Cara didn't think that mattered any more than the shoes being a couple sizes too large.

Both Holt and Hap stood up when she entered the room. Now Holt came forward with a crooked elbow. "Beautiful," he said. "Elegant. Perfect."

Cara beamed, and she kept beaming all through the evening.

The drive, filled with lighthearted conversation about Charlotte's recently improved sense of style, proved shorter than Cara expected. Perhaps, she mused, it had something to do with the company. Holt had made reservations at one of the finer restaurants in Lawton, so Cara soon found herself following a smiling young waitress through a dimly lit room tastefully decorated against a backdrop of oak planking and black lacquer. As they wound their way through tables dressed with black linens and red roses, Cara felt Holt behind her, his hand riding gently against the small of her back.

Compared to some of the restaurants Addison had frequented back in California, the place would probably be thought fairly pedestrian, but Cara appreciated the quiet atmosphere and the aura of privacy that came with it. Holt stepped up and quickly pulled out her chair for her as the waitress placed their menus on the table. Taking his seat opposite her, Holt laid aside his menu without even looking at it.

"You seem to know what you want," she noted, skimming her gaze over the heavy parchment page of her own menu.

"I do, yes."

She looked up into his warmly glowing eyes. Something shimmered between them, but she pushed it away. Best not to let her imagination run away with her. This amounted to an act of kindness on his part, not a declaration of romantic intent. She sat up a little straighter. "You've been here before then?"

"Nope." After a moment, he looked down, smoothing his napkin across his lap. "I took a look at the menu on the Internet."

"Ah."

He folded his hands together. "Had to be sure it was the right sort of place."

"The right sort of place for what?"

"For a beautiful woman and a special occasion."

Cara caught her breath. She dared not take his sweet words too seriously, however. They were not sweethearts. This was just Holt taking care of her as he took care of everyone around him. His kindness and generosity moved her, though, misting her eyes. She looked back to the menu, saying softly, "Thank you."

"It's my pleasure," he told her. "This is nice. To tell you the truth, I can't remember the last time Valentine's was anything but just another day to me."

Cara remembered all too well her last Valentine's Day. Hugely pregnant, she'd sat home alone while Addison had claimed to be entertaining important clients. He'd come in long after she'd gone to bed and seemed peeved in the morning because she hadn't been appropriately thrilled with the wilted bouquet of flowers that he'd left on the kitchen counter the night before. Even sitting here in a borrowed dress and shoes that were too large, she felt special and pampered by comparison.

She tried to derail those feelings, knowing that they were unwarranted and dangerous, but Holt's smile and easy manner disarmed her. Now that he knew her true identity, he'd been generous to a fault. She almost missed the old suspicious Holt. At least she'd had no doubt where she'd stood with him. If he ever learned the whole truth about her, his generosity and thoughtfulness would undoubtedly turn to disdain. She prayed that never happened.

After a leisurely dinner, Holt surprised Cara yet again by announcing that he had prepurchased movie tickets via the computer. As he escorted her out of the restaurant, he remarked repeatedly that he hoped he'd made a good choice. Nothing she said seemed to lessen his concern on that score.

Once they arrived at the movie theater, Cara began to understand where that surprising angst came from, as it quickly became evident that he'd never laid eyes on the place before. He seemed somewhat befuddled by the electronic ticket checker and a tad overwhelmed by the multiple offering of the many screens. Finally, they found the correct theater and excused their way past a long row of early arrivals to take the only pair of remaining seats.

The film, a comedy, kept them both in stitches. It was not one that Cara would have chosen, but she found it surprisingly charming, almost as charming as the man at her side. Once as they were both reeling with laughter, their shoulders collided. Holt casually slid his arm around her, and there it stayed. She refused to read anything into that, but she could not deny that she felt protected, even perhaps, just a little bit, treasured.

They left the theater chuckling over their favorite bits, so the ride home began in laughter. As talk dwindled, however, Holt switched on the radio, filling the truck with dreamy music fit for the occasion. By the time they arrived back at the motel, Cara floated on a sea of relaxed delight.

Holt accompanied her as far as the kitchen, but there in the dark, he drew her to a halt, pulling her into his arms. She went willingly, no longer able to pretend that the occasion and the evening had not affected them. Her heart clutched tight in a fist of emotion. She told herself that she deserved this moment, to believe in the possibility of romance. What if… But good sense refused to be ignored. A man like Holt did not indulge himself frivolously, and he might well regret this one small incident.

"Holt," she whispered, "are you sure about this?"

He pressed a finger to her lips. "I've already said everything there is to say to myself about it."

"In that case…" She twined her arms around his neck, lifting her face. "Thank you for tonight."

They kissed for a long while. It wrapped around them like a warm blanket, that kiss, bundling them together in a way that neither could quite explain. Afterward, they simply stood together, her head tucked beneath his chin. Finally, he pulled away, leaving her there in the warm, silent darkness, at peace for the first time in far, far too long.

It wouldn't last, of course. Sunday's sermon brought the same crushing sense of guilt that had haunted Cara from the first, and Wednesday's prayer service left her once more in silent, aching tears that seemed to destroy the careful, joyful truce in which she and Holt had been operating. He grew frustrated with her on the way home to Ace and Hap, who had stayed in because his arthritis had worsened with the continuing cold weather.

"Why can't you get it through that pretty little head of yours that I only want to help?" Holt demanded of her as they swept into the apartment through the kitchen door. She only shook that "pretty little head," biting her tongue against a snappish reply, before walking straight into disaster.

Chairs scraped back from the far side of the table, a figure rose, leaving Hap seated in his usual chair, a worried expression on his long, weathered, beloved face.

"Cara, honey," he rasped. "This fellow says he's come to take you and Ace back to California. I told him there must be some mistake."

Cara stared into the glittering eyes of her brother, and a scream gathered in her chest, a wail of grief and betrayal, but she locked it inside. She had known. All along she had known that it would come to this. Her sins had finally caught up with her.

Chapter Fifteen

"No mistake," Eddie said, grinning like the scheming cad he was. "Right, sis?"

"How did you find me?" she asked with the calm that came from accepting one's doom.

Eddie smugly rocked back on his heels. As usual, he wore too much cologne and a cheap, orangey-tan jacket over rust-colored pants and a matching T-shirt, his light brown hair slicked back from his face to curl at his nape.

"Wasn't so tough. Couldn't be any doubt where you'd head. I just drove by Aunt Jane's old house, and this nice young couple there told me a guy had come by looking for information." He slid a glance a Holt, who seemed frozen in place. "Said he wore a cap with a company logo and the words 'Jefford Exploration' on it. Took a little while to put two and two together and come up with the Heavenly Arms Motel." He looked around him then, a thinly veiled sneer curling his lips. "You come down in the world, sis."

"Don't you dare!" Cara hissed angrily.

"Seems to me we ought to take this to the front room before someone accidentally wakes our boy," he said.

"Our boy?" Eddie queried avidly. "Ace is here?"

"Of course Ace is here!" Cara snapped. "Where else would he be except with his mother? Where he belongs."

"Well, now," Eddie said. "That's a matter of opinion, isn't it?"

She had no doubt of Eddie's opinion on the matter. Sick with dread and dismay, she made herself face Hap. "Actually, if you don't mind, I'd like to speak to my brother in private."

Hap glanced at Holt, who took a half step forward. After a moment, Hap nodded. "You just holler if you need anything."

She turned away, intending to take Eddie out the back through the kitchen and across the lot to her old room, where they could be assured of privacy. Perhaps, she thought wildly, if she could just keep him quiet for a bit, put him off somehow, she might find a moment to run. Sickened at the prospect, she could not so much as look at Holt, even when his hand shot out and fastened around her wrist.

"Cara? Are you sure about this?"

Eddie appeared in front her, wearing his jolly, buddy-to-the-world smile. "Hey, I'm her brother, man. Didn't she ever mention old Eddie?"

"Is that true? Is he your brother?"

"Yes, unfortunately, he is."

"He-e-ey," Eddie protested mildly.

Flaying him with her gaze, Cara ground out, "Just don't let him anywhere near my son."

"Don't worry," Holt said, releasing her.

She finally chanced a glance in his direction and found him staring a threat at Eddie. She loved him for that. Who was she kidding? She'd loved Holt for a long time already. This just gave her one more reason to regret whatever must come, one more way to break her heart.

Brushing past Eddie, she led the way out of the apartment.

He made comments about the weather—too gray and too cold—as they crossed to the room. She let him in, then stood back and waited.

"Man," Eddie said, turning in a slow circle in the midst of her room. He shook his head, looking up at her from beneath the rise of his brow. "Even the clinic beats this dump, wouldn't you say?"

"No, I wouldn't," Cara told him. "Not that it matters. I'm not going back."

He shrugged and slid his hands into the pockets of his slacks, sneering down at the sofa as if to say he wouldn't dare sit there. "Not willingly, maybe."

Chilled, Cara folded her arms. "You can't make me go back, Eddie."

"No," he conceded, his tone light, unconcerned. "But the Elmonts can." He pegged her with a look then. "They've got a commitment order, Cara. They can come after you anytime they want. But it's not too late."

"I'm not going back," she repeated, hating the hint of desperation in her tone.

"We can still fix this. All the Elmonts care about is getting their grandson back. You come with me and everyone wins."

Cara let out a bark of derisive laughter. "And how do you figure that, Eddie? I really want to know."

"Simple." He spread his hands. "We negotiate a nice settlement, with visitation rights, for guardianship, and Ace grows up in the lap of luxury. That's better than them winning full custody in court, isn't it? I can even fix it so you don't have to go back to the clinic."

"That's very big of you, Eddie," she said sarcastically. "And just what is it that you get out of this benign arrangement?"

He waved a manicured hand. "Man's got to earn a living. You cut me in on the settlement, say fifty-fifty." He looked her in the eye then, adding, "Or there's always the finder's fee. Your choice."

"The Elmonts have offered a reward," she guessed, not at all surprised.

"Chicken feed compared to what we can take them for," he said urgently.

"You mean for what we can sell my son for!" she erupted.

He shrugged, cool as a cucumber. "Call it what you want. They're just two loving grandparents willing to give up a fortune to insure the well-being of their only heir."

"What?" Cara gasped. "Their *only* heir?"

"Didn't you know? They cut out Addison and his sister the day he told them you were pregnant. They always intended to raise the boy. Addison would have arranged it himself if he hadn't died like that."

"For a price, no doubt!" Cara spat, reeling. Was there no limit to her late husband's greed and self-centeredness?

"Look, you can't blame Addison," Eddie said. "You know how the Elmonts are."

"Controlling, manipulative. They have to own everything and everyone around them."

"And they've got the money to do it," Eddie confirmed. "But, hey, beats a shabby fourth-floor walk-up and an old lady more concerned about her next fix than dinner, you know? At least, that's the way I figure it."

"You talk like it has to be one or the other," Cara argued. "Didn't Aunt Jane show you that there's another way?"

"Aunt Jane," Eddie scoffed. "What was it about her that got to you? She never had anything in her whole life, not even her own kids."

"She had love, Eddie. She had love to give."

"Love," Eddie echoed dismissively. "That and five bucks will get you a decent cup of coffee." He waved a hand.

"Well, it doesn't matter now. Old girl's gone, and the Elmonts are coming." He thumped himself in the chest. "I'm your best shot of staying out of the loony bin now, kid, and you know it." He winked and added, "Has old Eddie ever steered you wrong?"

Cara shook her head, not in answer to his question, but in wonder that he had never appreciated what Aunt Jane had offered them, someone to love and be loved by. That and that alone had saved her from following in their mother's footsteps. Maybe that was all she really had to offer her son, too, but it would be more than the Elmonts could give him with all their money.

"You think about it," Eddie said, patting her shoulder.

Those were the same words he'd used when urging her to date Addison way back when, though she'd known even then that she was too young, too vulnerable. She had listened to him once, but never again. Poor Eddie. He just didn't understand that he'd used up every bit of his credibility with her then.

He moved to the door, saying, "I'm going to find me a bite to eat. Then we'll talk again." He wagged a finger at her. "You think on it, and then you'll know I'm right."

With that, he went out the door, leaving her to fall to her knees in silent, frenzied supplication.

"I'm telling you, it's a wonder they didn't cart her off in a straitjacket," Eddie said, shaking his head. "Wailing and screeching. I mean, okay, it was a shock. The man was dead." Eddie shuddered. "Falling like that." He bounced his shoulders up and down as if shaking off the willies. "Let that be a lesson to you, hey? Don't stop on an overpass to help some chick change a flat. I mean, call a wrecker, for pity's sake. Right? Am I right?"

From his seat on the edge of one of the black leather couches in the front room, Holt traded a significant look with his grandfather, ignoring Eddie's question—and everything else about the man that he could. Holt feared that if he paid too much attention to Cara's brother, he'd rearrange Eddie's face for him.

"So you're telling us that Cara's in-laws had her committed because of her grief over her husband's death?" he probed.

"Well, no, not right away. She went into the clinic willingly at first."

"At first."

"Yeah, you know, because of the shock."

"Of her husband's death."

"That and finding out she didn't have any place to live, I guess."

"No place to live?" Hap asked, tilting his rocking chair forward. "Why wouldn't she have anyplace to live?"

"Because the house belonged to the Elmonts," Eddie said, as if it were the only sane assumption.

Holt bowed his head, remembering what she'd said about that the day he'd taken her out to his place. She'd been so impressed by what he'd built for himself, what no one could take away from him. When he thought about how hard she'd fought to claim that little kitchenette out back for her and Ace… He swallowed and sucked in a deep, calming breath.

"Look, she's my sister and all," Eddie went on in that insufferably reasonable tone of his, "but you can understand why the Elmonts want custody of their grandson. It's a wonder they didn't cart her off in a straitjacket that day, and it's not like they wouldn't let her ever see Ace again."

Holt tamped down his temper. "Uh-huh."

"Between you and me," Eddie went on, sliding to the edge of his seat and leaning forward, "there's a reward. Twenty-five grand. I wouldn't bring it up, but you've been so good to her, hiring her off the street and all. And after the way she's had you on—Cara Jane Wynne, hoo, boy—you ought to have something for your trouble." He sat back and crossed his legs, pinching the crease in his slacks. "I'll hook you up with that. Be glad to do it."

"And what about your sister?" Hap demanded, clearly wondering if he'd heard right.

"Don't worry about her," Eddie counseled. "I'll negotiate a generous settlement for her."

"In return for custody of Ace," Holt said, his temper beginning to slip.

"They'll send her back to that clinic," Hap declared, looking to Holt.

"She'll be well taken care of," Eddie confirmed.

Holt pushed up to his full height. "I see."

Eddie smiled. "I knew you'd get it. Cara would, too, if she was in her right mind."

"There's just one thing I don't understand," Holt said.

"What's that?"

"How is it, with everything that she's been through, Cara turned out to be so sweet and hardworking and good," Holt asked, calmly reaching down to yank Eddie up by his shirt collar, "while you became such a creep?"

"Hey!" Flailing his arms, Eddie resisted only minimally as Holt propelled him toward the door.

Hap, bless him, rocked up to his feet and hobbled swiftly across the room. "Here, let me help you." He shoved open the door, grinning at Holt as he thrust Eddie through it. "Interesting to meet you, Mr. Sharp," Hap called as the door swung closed. "Real interesting. What do we do now?" he asked Holt, ignoring Eddie's indignant shouts.

Holt glanced at the door. "You mean, since we can't give Eddie Sharp the beating he deserves?"

"More's the pity," Hap grumbled. He shook his head. "Poor girl. She can't fight folks like that on her own."

Holt grinned. "Which is surely why God gave Ty all that money."

"And gave us Ty!" Hap added, laughing. He pulled himself up straight.

"I'll go find Cara while you call him," Holt said, heading for the apartment.

Hap turned toward the office, chuckling. "Them Elmonts just *think* they got money."

"And Eddie Sharp isn't." Sharp, that was. In fact, unlike his sister, Eddie Sharp couldn't have been much duller.

He found her on her knees, weeping. Pulling her up, he sat her on the couch, dried her tears and sat beside her.

"Where's Eddie?" she asked, sniffing.

"On his way to California by now, if he knows what's good for him."

She scoffed. "Eddie always knows what's good for him. But what makes you think he'd leave?"

"I threw him out."

She goggled at him. "You did what?"

"Threw him out. It's the least I could after I led him right to you," he muttered.

"Don't blame yourself for that," she said, wincing. "You wouldn't have gone there if I hadn't lied to you. Thank you for getting rid of him, by the way."

"Actually, Hap helped. He opened the door."

Her jaw dropped. When Holt told her what Eddie had said, though, she began crying again. What could he do but put an arm around her?

"No, no. It's all right. I only want to hear your side of the story now."

She told him in fits and starts between tears and fortifying breaths. They had delivered the news of Addison's death in one breath and told her that she would have to leave her home in the next. Ace, they had said, could stay with them. Tired from having struggled through the night alone with a colicky infant, Cara had simply come apart.

"I couldn't think, couldn't take it all in."

Holt shook his head and pulled her close against his side. "Who could blame you?"

She had gone of her own accord with the doctor summoned by her in-laws, and that, she said, had been her first mistake. "I thought it would appease them and give me somewhere private to get over my grief while I figured out what to do."

They'd brought a nurse to care for Ace. It hadn't occurred to her that they meant to keep him, until her "temporary respite" had turned into an actual commitment.

"They told me that I had no choice, that it would look better if I signed the papers rather than forced them to petition the court on my behalf. I decided to go along, thinking I'd get back home to my son sooner that way."

"So you essentially committed yourself for treatment," Holt surmised.

"Yes. Later, when I was served with papers saying that the Elmonts had filed for full custody of Ace, I realized what a mistake I'd made."

Her protests had only made matters worse.

"If I gave in to my anger, they told me I was behaving unreasonably. If I wept, they concluded I was depressed. When I begged, they essentially patted me on the head and told me to concentrate on 'getting better.'"

"And meanwhile, the Elmonts had your son."

Eventually Cara had learned to play the game, to give the staff at the private hospital what they wanted in order to "progress." She'd finally won supervised visits with her growing son, and then, thanks to an astute and sympathetic social services caseworker, weekends and holidays spent with him at the Elmont home. But the deck had been stacked against her, and with no financial resources to enable her to fight via the courts, Cara had done the only thing she could do; she'd run.

"I stashed what clothing I could for the two of us, whatever wouldn't be missed."

Holt chuckled and shook his head. "No wonder you showed up outfitted for the summer. What I don't understand is how you managed to fake your identity."

It seemed simple when she explained it. "I'd once overheard Addison mention a man in Oregon who could provide fake documents. So that's where I headed first."

In an unguarded moment, she'd taken Ace, jumped into the minivan that the Elmonts had deemed appropriate for a mother and driven north. Once there, she'd sold the van and used the money to buy a used car and false documents.

"My husband did me two favors," she said. "Three, counting Ace."

"He told you where to get a driver's license and Social Security card with your aunt's name on them," Holt surmised.

Nodding, she added, "And he put the minivan in my name. It wasn't cool enough for him to own, you see. Oh, he acted all magnanimous about it, pretended that buying it was all his idea, but I knew the Elmonts had purchased it as a reward for us providing them with a grandchild."

Armed with a new identity, she'd struck out for Oklahoma, the only haven she'd ever truly known. Realizing that Eddie would surely think to look for her around Duncan, she'd chosen Eden, based on its name alone.

"Just picked it out on a map. How stupid was that?"

"Not at all," Holt told her. "I suspect God was guiding you even then."

"I don't know about that," she said, shaking her head. "I just couldn't let the Elmonts raise my son. He'd turn out just like his father, dancing to the Elmont tune, willing to do anything for a buck, building his life on shallow image and foolish ideas of success."

"You did the right thing," Holt told her.

She looked at him in surprise. "You think so?"

"Absolutely."

She stared at him for several moments before giving her head a decisive nod. "My one regret, really, is that I have to do it again."

He pulled back a little, frowning down at her in confusion. "Do what again?"

She turned woeful eyes up to him. "Surely you see that I have no choice. I have to disappear before the Elmonts get to us."

"No," he said, quite calmly, he thought.

"I can't let them take Ace!" she exclaimed, leaping to her feet.

"Of course you can't," Holt agreed, rising to face her.

"But how can I fight them?"

"We," Holt corrected. "The question is, how can *we* fight them? And the answer is, with every resource at our disposal."

"You don't hate me?"

"Hate you? Of course I don't hate you." He watched hope blossom in those soft gray eyes before they slowly filled with tears again. "It's okay," Holt promised. "It's all going to work out."

"It's not that," she squeaked.

"Then what is it?"

She swiped at the tears streaming down her face, and choked out, "Grover."

"What about Grover?"

"I'm ready," she managed, gripping his sleeve. "I'm finally ready to say that prayer."

She covered her face with her hands and sobbed. Holt pulled out his cell phone. He couldn't be certain what this was about, but he had the feeling that Grover would know. As for himself, he had no doubt that he'd do anything she asked of him from now on, importune Ty on her behalf, summon the pastor, pray the moon down right out of the sky, whatever she needed.

In a way, he felt an immense relief. The secrets had been uncovered, and knowing why she'd done what she had, he couldn't fault her. Indeed, he applauded her courage and initiative. Yes, he feared for her, too, but he trusted that right and truth would win out, with God's help, and surely God was with them.

Cara might not think so now, but Holt would forever believe that God had guided her eyes the day she'd perused that map and let her gaze settle on Eden. He had no doubt at all himself now. He should have trusted, the very first day that she'd walked into the place, that she was the answer to all his prayers.

Grover arrived within minutes. Cara and Holt barely beat him to the lobby. She went at once to her knees, so anxious was she to unburden herself fully at last, barely noticing when Hap handed Holt the house phone. With Grover and Hap beside her, she spilled her sins at God's feet, begging His forgiveness. She dared not ask for His help, after all that she'd done. It was enough that Holt and Hap seemed willing to forgive her and lend their aid.

She still couldn't believe that, in the end, she wouldn't have to pack up and flee with her son. Eddie would be back, and the Elmonts wouldn't be far behind him. But she wouldn't think of that just now. Nothing mattered just then but unburdening her heart and, at long last, getting right with God. The rest could wait. For a bit.

After several minutes of conversation with Grover and then more prayer, during which she did ask Jesus into her heart, vowing her belief and acceptance, Grover tried to give her reason for hope.

"You're not alone now, Cara. Never again. And you need not have waited. God knows your heart, honey. He knows you acted out of fear and concern. Even now the Holy Spirit is lifting up your troubles to the heavenly Father with groans too deep for simple words. He'll work this out. You'll see."

"He already is," Holt announced, appearing in front of her. He squatted at her feet, bringing himself eye level with her as she sat on the couch between Hap and Grover. "I just got off the phone with Tyler. He'll have an attorney for us in the morning."

Cara put a hand to her head, teetering on the edge of relief so great it seemed unbelievable on one hand and a world of all-too-familiar concern on the other. "I—I can't pay a lawyer."

"Not to worry," Holt stated flatly.

Cara shook her head. "You don't understand. The Elmonts have money, enough to make it very, very expensive to fight them."

Holt just smiled. "You don't understand. Tyler says he can't contribute more than a couple million to start, but that we should give him a few days."

"A couple million!" Cara yelped.

Holt shook his head. "Personally, I don't think it's going to take anything like that, but let's talk to the attorney before we reign him in. Okay?"

Several seconds ticked by before she could wrap her mind around what was happening, and even then she couldn't quite believe it. "But why?"

"Why what?"

"Why would Tyler do such a thing?"

Holt traded looks with Hap, who rasped, "Why, because he can. What else is all that money for, after all, if not to do good?"

"But why do this for *me?*" she persisted.

"Because we asked him to," Holt said bluntly.

"But I lied to you!" she argued. "I used you."

"I don't see how you used us," Hap rasped, shaking his head. "You've done more than your fair share of work around here, more even than what we hired you for."

"As for the other," Holt said, "you only did what you felt you had to do. No fault in that."

Stunned, Cara could only gape at him for long moments, and then she began to sob again, too grateful for words. She knew that the nightmare had not ended, only taken an unexpected turn, but to her everlasting relief, no one even mentioned calling a doctor.

Chapter Sixteen

Holt turned the truck into a small, old-fashioned gasoline station. Flanked by a sheet metal fence meant to conceal a salvage yard and boasting only two pumps and a single garage bay, the circa 1950s building bore the title of Froggy's Gas & Tires. The place looked closed, however, and Cara had a difficult time believing that Holt had bullied her out into the cold just to show her where she could buy gas for her old car.

"What is going on?" she asked, the tension of the past two days making her tone more sharp than she'd intended.

"Distraction," Holt answered, driving right past the station and across the lot to a small clapboard house beyond. The light above the uncovered stoop came on as the truck drew to a halt. Holt killed the engine and shifted sideways in his seat, facing Cara. "Froggy and Kelly Priddy are friends of mine. You met them briefly at the Watermelon Patch."

"*Froggy?*"

"It's a nickname, but he prefers it to his given name of Filmore. He helped me fix your car, by the way."

"And we're here because of that?"

"We're here because we've been invited over, and I thought you could use the distraction, so I accepted."

Cara didn't know whether to be touched by Holt's concern for her state of mind or indignant at his high-handedness. Before she could decide what her reaction would be, the door of the tiny, hip-roofed house opened and a man appeared in the doorway. Squat and lipless, he'd obviously earned his unusual nickname by appearance, but the effusiveness of his greeting instantly endeared him to Cara, who set aside her irritation and followed Holt's lead by getting out of the car. Froggy jogged across the square stoop and down the steps to pound the much taller Holt on the back.

"Come on in out of the cold! Kelly's heated some cider. Got them fat little cinnamon sticks in it and everything."

He bounded back up the steps and into the house. Holt waited until Cara reached him, then climbed the three steep steps at her side and ushered her inside. Kelly Priddy met them with steaming cups containing the aforementioned cinnamon sticks. As plain as her tidy living room with its white walls and nondescript brown furnishings, Kelly stood perhaps an inch or two taller than her squat husband, her straight, light brown hair flowing over her plump shoulders. The bangs gave her a girlish air even before she giggled, showing front teeth with a slight gap between them.

In short order, Cara found herself seated next to Holt on the sofa while Froggy took the only chair and Kelly parked herself on the matching ottoman to one side. The television played softly in the background while they sipped their cider and chatted. Cara took the opportunity to thank Froggy for working on her car.

"Aw, Holt's helped me out more than once, I can tell you."

"Still, it was my car, and if I can ever repay the favor in any way," Cara began. At that point, Kelly bounced up to her feet and waved a hand at her, turning toward the open doorway between the living area and kitchen.

"Come tell me what you think about this."

With a bemused glance at Holt, Cara set her cup on the side table and rose to follow her hostess. A moment later, she found herself standing in a small eat-in kitchen. The square table and four chairs with red seat cushions had been shoved up against one wall to leave as much space as possible, but the room still felt crowded. Kelly regarded the window over the sink, or, rather, the colorful curtains hanging over that window. On closer inspection, Cara saw that the "curtains" were actually just lengths of fabric that had been draped over the rod.

"Coordinating or contrasting?" Kelly asked, tapping her forefinger against her chin.

Cara looked around the room again, noting the red towels that hung from the oven door handle and the red frame of the clock on the wall. "Coordinating," she decided, pointing to the cherry-print fabric in the center of the window rod. "But if you want contrast, you might try banding it in the yellow."

Kelly Priddy threw up her arms. "Brilliant! But why not the green?"

Cara tilted her head. "Too Christmasy for every day, don't you think?"

Kelly smacked herself in the middle of her bangs. "Duh. So, do you sew?"

Cara shook her head. "Never learned."

"I'll teach you," Kelly announced, reaching for a bowl of potato chips on the counter. "Let's give the guys some snacks, then I'll show you the bedroom so you can see what I've done in there." She winked at Cara and whispered, "Froggy likes a fancy boudoir. Romantic cuss."

Fancy turned out to be big flower prints, ruffles and lace. Cara managed to keep a straight face as Kelly explained how she'd created the various elements in the room. Amazed by the level of expertise in the workmanship if not the frilly decor, Cara soon found herself caught up in laughing conversation, which continued even after they rejoined the men. With every word and gesture, Kelly told Cara how much she adored her odd-looking husband. As the sentiment seemed entirely mutual, Cara could only envy the Priddys.

She and Holt departed several hours later with hugs from Kelly and handshakes from Froggy. "Good night, and thank you!" she called one more time as Holt handed her up into the passenger seat. When he slid beneath the wheel a few seconds later, she thanked him, too. "I guess I needed that to keep my mind off Eddie and the Elmonts," she admitted, "but next time try asking, why don't you?"

"Good advice," he said around a grin.

Too bad he didn't take it.

Five long days after Eddie blew her carefully constructed little world apart, Cara at last sat across the desk from one David Hyde in his Duncan law office, Holt beside her.

A stout man of middle height with frizzy gray hair, Hyde wore a huge college ring on one hand and a narrow wedding band on the other, along with golf clothes. Clearly they had interfered with his plans for the day, but he listened to the whole ugly story as if fully prepared to give them his undivided attention for as long as it took. After what felt like hours of questions, replies, notes and instructions via the intercom to his assistant in another room, the attorney gave it to them straight.

"I'm not familiar with California law. We're researching that now. But according to Oklahoma statutes, since the commitment was voluntary, we only have a few problems." He ticked them off, along with their possible solutions, everything from psychological evaluations to the most important consideration, a stable home environment for Ace. "For my money," he went on, looking them square in the eyes, "the easiest, quickest, most unassailable fix is for the two of you just to get married."

Cara bit her lips to prevent her gasp from escaping, while David Hyde went on, pointing out the obvious benefits of such an arrangement.

"It's one thing to fight a single woman for custody of her child," he concluded, "another to destroy a family. Make yourselves a family, and you've created a fortress of sorts. Then we fight from a strengthened position."

Finally, he sat back, waiting for their response.

Cara gulped, keenly aware of Holt's silent presence, and marshaled together the only possible reply. "I'm afraid you've misconstrued the relationship between Mr. Jefford and me."

"He's right, Cara," Holt interrupted, taking her hand. "Fighting a married couple is a whole lot different from bullying a single mother. We should think about this."

Appalled, she shook her head. Supporting her was one thing. Convincing his brother-in-law to bankroll her legal battles went far beyond anything she had a right to expect. She would not allow Holt to take this to absurd levels. She got to her feet as calmly as she could and stuck out her hand for Mr. Hyde.

"Thank you, sir. I feel much better knowing that you're on this."

"My pleasure," Hyde assured her, and she didn't doubt it a bit, considering what Tyler must be paying him. Holt, however, did not figure into this. How could anyone expect him to saddle himself with a wife and child just to help her win a custody suit?

Poor Holt. He'd only begun to make peace with the lies he'd known about when the whole truth had exploded in his face. She couldn't let his guilt at unwittingly leading Eddie to her dictate his future.

Though aching inside, she walked out with her head high and eyes dry. Later, when Holt broached the subject again, she had to turn her face away in order to maintain her composure.

"It makes sense, Cara."

"Not to me."

"Look, if getting married will put a stop to this nonsense—"

"This subject is closed," she interrupted sternly. "And that's all I have to say on the matter."

He gave up, and they drove back to Eden in silence.

Holt sat slumped over the dining table, his head in his hands. He felt all prayed out and still in shock over everything that had happened. He'd spent the first three of the past five days keeping Eddie Sharp away from Cara and Ace. Eddie had not, as hoped, returned to California, but he hadn't had enough nerve to approach Cara again, either. That respite, Holt knew, would not last. Time was running out. Eventually Eddie would give up and summon the Elmonts. It would undoubtedly be best, as Hyde had pointed out, if they were married before that happened. That way Holt could fight for her. Apparently, though, Cara just didn't see things that way. What hurt him most about that was the cool, resolute manner in which she had refused Hyde's suggestion.

"I'm afraid you've misconstrued the relationship between Mr. Jefford and me."

Holt had been shocked to hear Hyde's blunt suggestion that they marry, but he'd immediately seen the sense of it. In that moment, it had even seemed inevitable, the absolutely correct end to all that had gone on before, but it appeared that he had "misconstrued" the woman's feelings for him. After that meeting in the lawyer's office, Cara had refused even to discuss the idea of marriage to him, and that had hurt Holt right into his own silence.

Ryan clumped into the room. "There you are! Granddad and I were waiting for you to get back and tell us what the lawyer had to say. Where's Cara?"

"In her room."

"This doesn't sound good," Ryan muttered, coming to brace his hands on the back of the chair at the end of the table. "Tell me everything."

Holt did, including the lawyer's suggestion that he and Cara marry.

"So what's the problem?" Ryan asked, pulling out the chair and sitting down. Holt glared at him, partly in surprise, partly in anger. "Don't look at me like that," Ryan drawled, "and don't try to tell me you aren't wild about the girl. We've all seen it."

Holt felt his ears heat and quickly looked down at his hands. "It's not that simple."

"I don't see why not. Unless you've still got that stupid idea about the oil business being too dangerous for married men."

Holt stared more than glared this time.

"Did you think we didn't know?" Ryan chuckled and sat back, draping an arm over the back of the chair. "That's it, isn't it? Tell me something. When was the last time you or any of your men had to go up top on a rig?"

"Falling isn't the only danger," Holt grumbled. "We blew two full lengths of pipe recently."

"So? Everyone will be more careful now, won't they? Check everything twice, I'm sure." Holt looked away, because that was precisely what they were doing. "What about truck drivers, Holt? Lots more of them die every year than roughnecks. What about firemen? Policemen? Soldiers? Are those jobs only for single men? I don't think so."

Holt didn't think so, either. He knew his conviction about staying single had more to do with the grief and fear that he'd somehow held on to when he should have turned it over to God instead. That didn't solve anything, however.

"I'm not the issue. I made it clear I was willing to marry her."

Ryan reared back in his chair. "Willing? That must have thrilled Cara right down to her little bitty toes."

"Look," Holt snapped, "Cara is the one who doesn't want to marry me. All right?"

"Well, I don't know. Is it all right with you?"

"If that's the way she wants it," Holt muttered.

"What about what you want?"

"That apparently doesn't figure into it."

"Maybe she doesn't know how you feel about it."

"How could she not?" Holt demanded, surprised by his own anger. "After everything I've done, everything that's happened, how could she not know?" He rose, suddenly too worked up to stay in his chair. "I mean, I knew. Okay? I knew from the very beginning that she wasn't being truthful with us, but I kept it to myself."

"And why was that, I wonder?" Ryan asked.

"What difference does it make?" Holt retorted hotly. "She lied, and I kept mum. With every inconsistency that cropped up, I kept it to myself. I *protected* her!"

"Of course, you did," Ryan commented idly. "That's what you do, protect the people you care about."

"Exactly! And if that wasn't enough, what about after I found out she'd faked her identity? I kept quiet about that, too." He thumped himself in the chest. "I stood by her. Even though she wouldn't trust me with the truth, I stood by her! I'd still be keeping her secrets if not for that brother of hers. Then it all blows up, and what do I do? I get her every bit of help I can find her, that's what?" He folded his arms, finishing glumly, "And now that she's got the whole family in her corner, she doesn't need me anymore."

"So what are you saying?" Ryan asked. "That Cara's an un-scrupulous, immoral, ungrateful—"

"No!" Holt shouted, throwing up his hands. "You know better!"

"Then what's really keeping you and Cara apart?" Ryan demanded, slapping his hands down against the tabletop.

"She doesn't love me!" Holt roared, thinking it obvious. Ryan straightened. "She doesn't love me," Holt repeated miserably.

Ryan folded his arms, a smug look on his face. "Oh, really? And I suppose Cara told you that?"

"Don't be ridiculous."

"Oh. Of course. That would be too obvious. Like you telling her how much you love her and Ace."

Holt winced. "Just stop it."

"Better yet, you stop with this 'willing' nonsense and tell her how you really feel," Ryan said. "Now would be a good time."

With that he turned aside, revealing Cara in the open doorway to her bedroom, her eyes wide with shock as she clung to the casement, Ace on her hip. They were the two most precious things in his own personal world, Holt realized, and they just stood there staring at him.

Cara held on to the doorframe for support, her heart pounding so hard that it threatened to knock her off her feet.

Earlier, she'd lain on her bed with Ace sitting in the curve of her body and once again tearfully poured out her heart to God. The whole thing had felt a little shop worn, frankly, as if God had sat there on His throne shaking His head in strained patience, asking what more she wanted from Him. She'd wanted solutions; He'd given her solutions, and then she'd complained that they were not to her taste? She had wondered petulantly if having a husband who actually loved her was too much to ask. It had never occurred to her that Holt might be questioning her feelings for him.

"Is that what you think?" she asked. "That I don't love you? After everything you've done for us, h-how could I *not* love you?"

He spread his hands. "But you told the lawyer that he had misconstrued—"

"Your feelings!" she interrupted. "I was talking about *your* feelings."

"*My* feelings? Why do you think I was there with you? Why do you think I've done the things I've done, why I couldn't just let it go and tend to my own business?"

"Because that's just the kind of man you are, Holt," she said, "a good Christian man with a big heart and broad shoulders that you expect the whole world to lean on."

"Oh, please! I've followed you around like some pathetic, adoring hound." He shoved a hand through his hair. "Everyone else has seen it! Why not you?"

"Because I'm me," she said, thumping herself in the chest. "I'm the escapee from the loony bin, the liar, the schemer." She shook her head. "A lousy schemer, but a schemer, nonetheless. I'm not what you thought I was, Holt."

"No, you're not what I first thought you were," he admitted, "but you're twice what I dreamed about. You and Ace, you're more than I ever dared want, more than I ever dared ask for. And, the truth is, Cara, God brought you here *to me*. You're mine! And I'll be hanged if—"

She never knew what he'd be hanged for. She somehow got across the room before he could tell her, and then he didn't have to, not with words, because he was kissing her, both her and Ace wrapped in his strong arms.

At some point, Ryan began to laugh, prompting them to pull

apart enough for Cara to gaze up into Holt's warm green eyes. "I don't deserve you," she whispered.

"Hoo, I'd better marry you before you come to your senses," Holt crowed joyfully.

"I'm serious, Holt," she insisted solemnly. "I do love you. How could I not? After everything you've done, you're already my hero. But I don't want to be rescued. That's not what marriage is supposed to be."

"Sweetheart," he said, "it's not about that. I'd planned to ask you as soon as the other issues were resolved. Then when the attorney suggested it, I thought…I thought how wondrously God works, dropping my heart's desire right into my lap like that. Then when you just dismissed the whole idea out of hand, I can't tell you how disappointed I was."

"Oh, Holt. I couldn't bear the thought of forcing you into something you didn't want. I was afraid you felt guilty about leading Eddie to us when the fault was mine all along."

Cupping her face in his big, capable hands, he pressed her forehead to hers, saying, "It's not about fault, not yours, not mine. God's been in charge here all along, honey. God knew, even before I did, how much I wanted, needed, you and Ace. He gave you Eden for a destination. He put your finger on just the right spot on that map. And He made sure that I was desperate enough to hire you when you walked in right off the street. Did you get that? *I* need you."

"Good grief," Ryan quipped, "I think he's about to give up the big brother cape."

Cara giggled. Holt dropped his hands from her face, his arm sliding around her shoulders as he turned toward his brother. "Okay, so maybe I have a little bit of a big brother complex."

"Ya think?" Ryan stepped up and clapped Holt on the shoulder, adding, "That wasn't a complaint, by the way. No one's ever had a better big brother than you."

"Thanks," Holt drawled before dropping his gaze to Cara once more. "But that's not what this is about. That's not what *we* are about. My wanting to marry you doesn't have anything to do with heroics. This is about you and me belonging together."

"Amen," Ryan agreed. Reaching for Ace, he winked at Cara. "Personally, I've always thought what this family needed was a cute blond sister-in-law and an adorable nephew." With that, he hoisted a chuckling Ace over his head.

"Heh, watch it," Hap said, limping in from the front room. "That's my grandson you're tossing around like a sack of grain there."

Cara pulled away from Holt and went to Hap. "You heard."

He looped an arm around her, reaching out for Holt with the other. "I'm old, but I'm not deaf, sugar. I heard, and I just have one thing to say. Let's get this show on the road."

Laughing, Cara hugged him. Holt's long arms embraced them both. Ryan carried Ace over to get in on the action, beaming ear to ear. Cara had never felt so loved, so included, so much a part of a something, so right.

She understood now what God had been telling her earlier. Her every problem had been solved. Her prayers had already been answered, with blessing heaped upon blessing until all the world could not hold them as they spilled out and ran over. God had kept His hand on her all along, from the very beginning. The Elmonts were not a problem; they were just a means He had used to get her here, to this man and this family, where she belonged.

They planned the simplest of ceremonies for the following Saturday, the first day of March, delaying only that long so Charlotte and Ty could whisk down from Dallas to be there.

Charlotte, God love her, came on Thursday morning armed

with a trunkful of dresses. From that bounty, Cara chose a formfitting, cream-colored knit chemise with a flowing overlay of dusty pink lace, the sleeves of which ended in fluttery, bell-shaped cuffs. They dashed to Duncan for cream-colored heels and a simple bouquet of pink roses.

Only the day before that Holt had insisted on buying a lovely diamond solitaire to go with the simple gold bands he and Cara had chosen for wedding rings. He'd also come up with, all on his own, a handsome black suit, white shirt, black-and-red pin-striped tie and black cowboy boots. Most astonishingly, he'd managed an almost identical outfit for Ace.

Cara informed her brother by telephone on Friday morning of the impending nuptials. He did not offer to walk her down the aisle as he had at her first wedding. Indeed, she'd hung up while he was raving about the fortune that could still be wrangled from the Elmonts, if only she'd "listen to reason."

How the whole of Eden had gotten the news about the wedding, Cara didn't know, but when she showed up at the church with Charlotte and Ty, who had dismissed her effusive thanks for his generosity with a heartfelt hug, the parking lot literally overflowed. Cars lined both sides of the streets in every direction. Cara couldn't have been more pleased. She only hoped that the ladies of the church, who had volunteered to prepare a meal for the reception, had gotten together enough food for all these people.

The only sad moment of the morning had come when Holt had sent in a copy of the Duncan paper, folded to the page that contained the obituary of Mrs. Poersel. Yet, it somehow seemed fitting that their wedding should take place on the same day as the old dear's funeral. Cara's only regret was that she and Holt couldn't be there. She didn't think her aunt's old friend would mind.

Now she stood with Charlotte in the freshening breeze, the barest hint of spring ruffling their skirts, and at last felt the serenity of that golden haven she had come seeking. Cara stepped off toward the church, and Ty rushed forward to open the door to her future.

Charlotte looked resplendent in a pale, minty suit that brought out the green flecks in her hazel eyes, her long auburn hair hanging down her back. Cara had twisted her own hair into a sleek roll on the back of her head, anchored with pink rose buds and white baby's breath. Charlotte had loaned her a set of genuine pearls for jewelry.

Having agreed to act as Cara's matron of honor, Charlotte preceded her down the aisle at a stately pace. They had chosen to forgo music, but Hap was there to escort Cara, his eyes misty and his dentures on display. Ryan, whose single duty as best man was to hold Ace, stood next to Holt before the altar.

Grover made an eloquent business of the rites, but both Cara and Holt were content to repeat the time-honored vows without inventive deviation or embellishment, while Froggy Priddy slipped around with a camera in his role of self-appointed photographer. Afterward, neither could stop smiling as they stood together in an impromptu reception line while their uninvited but very welcome guests streamed past them at the front of the church to the fellowship hall beyond. The very last to offer his congratulations turned out to be, to their surprise, none other than David Hyde, the attorney.

"Tyler didn't think you'd mind my showing up," he said, "especially since this seems like such a good time to give you this. It came by special messenger this morning."

Cara watched as he pulled an envelope from his inside coat pocket and handed it to her. A glance at the return address showed it to be from her former in-laws, but to her surprise, the envelope was addressed to Holt. Curiosity more than anything else piqued her interest, but she dutifully handed over the letter to her new husband.

Holt considered but a moment before tearing open the envelope and removing two pieces of paper. He glanced at the smaller of the two before passing it to Cara, who quickly realized that she held in her hand a check for twenty-five thousand dollars. That "finder's fee" of which Eddie had spoken! She digested that while Holt quickly read the letter, which he then handed back to Hyde.

"What does it say?" she asked, passing the check back to the attorney, too.

Holt slid his arm around her waist. "They respectfully request that I urge you to consider a formal visitation agreement, a very generous one. For them." He smiled down at her. "So they can see their grandson and heir."

Cara closed her eyes and leaned into him. It was over. She'd won. They'd won. Ace would grow up with every advantage that a loving Christian home could provide.

"I suppose the check is their way of sweetening the deal," Holt said with a chuckle, pulling her close. "As if it could get any sweeter."

"What should I tell them?" David Hyde asked, tucking the folded letter back into the pocket from which it came.

Cara looked at her husband and smiled. "Tell them we'll pray about it."

Nodding, Hyde held up the check. "And this?"

Holt shrugged. "I don't know." He looked down at Cara. "What do you think, wife?"

She considered. "Well, you did find me. Sort of."

"And I'm keeping you," he declared, pulling her closer still. She laughed and kissed his cheek. "Hey, maybe we should send it to Eddie," he said. "I mean, fair's fair, don't you think?"

"Poor Eddie," Cara said. "I'd hate to think that was all he'd get out of this."

"It does seem like a pittance compared to what we have, doesn't it?" Holt said.

Cara looked to David Hyde. "Make it our wedding gift to him, then."

Hyde just smiled and shook his head before slipping the check into his coat and walking away.

In the moment they had to themselves, before good manners would compel them to join the reception in the fellowship hall, Cara laid her head on her husband's shoulder and thought about what he'd just done, how easily he'd let go of that check. She knew that her son, not to mention her heart, would always be safe with Holt.

My hero, she thought, just before she winged a prayer of humble gratitude and growing wonder heavenward.

"Ready to celebrate, Mrs. Jefford?" he asked, folding her arm around his.

"With you," she answered. "Always."

* * * * *

*Take one more trip to Eden, OK,
in February 2009,
when brother Ryan gets his happily-ever-after in
THEIR SMALL-TOWN LOVE,
only from Love Inspired.*

Dear Reader,

Have you ever allowed guilt to separate you from God's blessings? I have—while God stood ready to supply my needs! All He requires is that we let go and let Him. As both Cara and Holt discover, that seems difficult—until we understand what we're holding on to instead of God.

Are you holding on to guilt, fear, pride, pain or intentions/goals instead of God? Guilt can be deserved, fear justified, pride misplaced, pain real, intentions good, but anything that keeps us from letting go and letting God is harmful.

As Scripture says, let us conquer our woes overwhelmingly through Him. Sometimes that means laying it all on the line for truth, which is precisely what must happen in the final book of this series, *Their Small-Town Love,* coming in February 2009. I hope you will enjoy Ryan and Ivy's journey to love and truth.

God bless,

Arlene James

QUESTIONS FOR DISCUSSION

1. What does it mean to conquer difficulties through Christ? (See Romans 8.) What did it mean in Cara's case? In Holt's?

2. Holt is an active Christian; in light of that, is Holt's suspicion of Cara understandable? Necessary? Why or why not?

3. None of Cara's clothes are appropriate for Oklahoma weather. Would this make you suspicious of who she is and where she came from? Why or why not?

4. Holt's grandfather Hap welcomes Cara, a stranger, into their lives. Would you be as welcoming of a stranger as he? Why or why not?

5. Cara believes that she cannot publicly confess her deception, and therefore cannot receive God's forgiveness. Do you agree?

6. Exodus 20:1—17 and Deuteronomy 5:6—21 give us what we know as the Ten Commandments. Exodus 20:16 and Deuteronomy 5:20 use the same words to convey what we think of as the ninth commandment—"You shall not bear false witness against your neighbor." Does Cara break this commandment? Why or why not?

7. What impact does Aunt Jane have on Cara? Why does her influence not lead Cara to a full understanding of the mission of Christ? Should it have?

8. Holt eventually comes to realize that he continues to allow himself to be affected by his past. Has this ever happened to you? What did you do to change things?

9. Cara is extremely protective of her son, Ace, going so far as to carry him on her back when she's cleaning motel rooms. Is she justified in doing so? What would you have done in her position?

10. Because Holt is an oil rigger, he believes that this prevents him from getting married and having a family. Do you agree with him? Why or why not?

11. Does Holt's visit with Mrs. Poersel soften him toward Cara's situation? How?

12. Cara assumes that Holt wants to marry her in order to provide protection for her and her son. Is this an acceptable reason for marriage? Why or why not?